All rights reserved, no part of this publication may be reproduced or transmitted by any means whatsoever without the prior permission of the publisher.
Text and Images © Kathy Sharp
Front cover created using public domain images modified by
Diane Narraway.
Edited by Veneficia Publications
&
Fi Woods

Typesetting © Veneficia Publications
VENEFICIA PUBLICATIONS UK
July 2022
veneficiapublications.com

Best wishes
Kathy Sharp

Call of the Merry Isle

by

Kathy Sharp

Once upon a time there was a young man who didn't quite know where he was going in life. Nothing unusual in that, you say. But in the dimension in which he lived, there were, shall we say, extra complications that the rest of us don't have to cope with. Allow me to tell you the whole story ...

CONTENTS

1: A bit of A Frolic	1

2: The Isle of No Such Place	10

3: The Words on the Window	19

4: The Merry Isle	25

5: The Know-It-All Inn	32

6: A Tempting Offer	40

7: The Sprit of the Sea	45

8: Paved with Pearls	50

9: Vocation, Vocation, and, er Vocation	62

10: The Talkative Mr Bliss	69

11: Merry Serpents	80

12: The Other World	90

13: Parchwell	104
14: Cast Adrift	112
15: Far Flung	118
16: Voyage of the Piddock	127
17: Larus Waits	137

A Bit of a Frolic

'My boy,' said Father Ormerod, with one of his annoying twinkles, 'however long you may chance to live, you will never be older than you are now.'

Patience Pontius, Reverend, newly ordained, goggled at that. He wondered whether to ask if it was a riddle. It sounded like a riddle.

Why couldn't people just say straightforward things? He never knew what to make of it when people spoke in roundabout language. And he could definitely do without the annoying twinkles. Was it a joke? Was it intended to be taken seriously? The young Reverend Pontius had no idea. He settled on a sort of half-smirk, somewhere between seeing the joke and being grateful for the insight, though he didn't and wasn't.

Father Ormerod shook his head. What would become of the boy? No insight at all, and as grave and as old as the hills in his earnestness. 'I've taught you all I can,' he said. 'It's time now for you to go out into the world. But I suggest you begin by indulging in a bit of a frolic first. It'll do you good.' This last was accompanied by another annoying twinkle.

The young Reverend Pontius goggled yet again. A *frolic*? Whatever could that mean? He looked carefully at Father Ormerod, hoping for a clue. Was this supposed to be another joke? In his mind, he pictured Father Ormerod turning away and kicking his heels as he went. Is that the kind of thing he meant? After all, looking at Mrs Ormerod, one couldn't imagine *her* offering to be *frolicsome.*

Life was such a puzzle. When he had entered the college, full of good intentions, Pontius had imagined he would learn the answers to things, rather than face ever-more peculiar questions. He had expected to come out feeling he was in the confidence of the Spirit of the Sky, but that deity still seemed as remote and mysterious as ever. And he couldn't, by the way, imagine the Spirit indulging in *frolics*. He had a feeling life in the clergy was going to turn out a lot stranger than he had anticipated.

Father Ormerod gave the young man a formal bow and turned away. 'A keen mind,' he muttered, 'but no sense at all. Perhaps not suited to the clergy. I give it a year, and he'll either settle to it, or concede defeat.'

But the good Father had underestimated his young charge. Pontius was nothing if not determined. Oh, he had the intensity of a terrier once he got his teeth into something and giving up was a notion that rarely occurred to him. He would bash his way through all obstacles in the service of the Spirit of the Sky. Little did he know just how many obstacles would be placed in his way, though, beginning with inexplicable advice to have a bit of a frolic.

※

It was surprising how often the notion of frolics recurred in the life of the young Reverend Pontius, however hard he tried to avoid them. And believe me, he had tried, regardless of Father Ormerod's advice. He had spent his free time in the college library, studying "improving" books. He chose his reading matter with great care. Not that you would expect to find anything contentious in the library of a theological college, of course, but you could never be sure what might have found its way in when the librarian's attention was distracted. He had one or two eyebrow-raising moments, nonetheless, when opinions varied from book to book, but these were mainly practical matters. None of them were things he would hesitate to debate with Father Ormerod, which he occasionally did. His mentor usually won, while managing to display a broad-minded tolerance of differing viewpoints. Pontius greatly enjoyed the cut and thrust of gentle argument even though he expected to lose. It helped to make things crystal-clear, and that made him happy. Father Ormerod never again suggested any frolicking, thankfully, and Pontius was grateful for that. However, the idea seemed to lodge stubbornly in the back of his mind, ambushing him when he least expected it.

'Unseemly,' he said, as he dressed himself one morning, when the word *frolic* had popped into his head yet again. 'Not a proper topic for a man of the cloth.'

He was putting on a very modest black frock coat and breeches, his second-best silk stockings, and his silver-buckled shoes. Were the silver buckles too much, he wondered? A little showy? Maybe not for church use, but Pontius was not going to church. He was going to see a lady. A young lady. His cheeks burned with the embarrassment of it. But this was something that had to be done, and it called for a middle line between sobriety and smartness. The buckles were on the smart side of the equation.

Better not think on it too deeply. A young clergyman would always be a man in want of a wife. Wives could undertake some of the work of a parish. Well, quite a lot of it, in all honesty. She would share the burden, at the very least, and obviate the need to employ a housekeeper. People always spread rumours about single gentlemen with housekeepers, didn't they? And though Pontius did not yet have a parish of his own, it was certainly not too soon to consider the options wife-wise. Miss Cynthia was easily the best bet so far: modest, quiet, accomplished in the right sort of way. Brought up in a frugal family by a strict mother. Much to be said for that, thought Pontius approvingly, as he set out.

An hour later, he was sitting on the tasteful bench in the garden of her parents' house trying, and mostly failing, to make suitable small talk. It was a beautiful garden, and it always distracted him. It had been the highlight of his several visits to Cynthia and her family. No doubt about it, he had looked at the garden more than he had looked at her. She had sat beside him in appreciative silence each time, as he pointed out an admirable shrub, or a pleasing leaf-shape, or a useful herb, as if those things had never occurred to her. She had nodded encouragingly, but said nothing much at all, for which he had mostly been grateful. But today was different. This day was an important step forward in life, one of the building blocks of his future. That thought was comforting. Building blocks were nice solid, practical things. But it was not a building block sitting on the bench beside him, it was a real live young woman. She wasn't stunningly pretty—that would have floored him—but just neatly attractive, which was perfect for what he had in mind. But to put what he had in mind into practice, he had to speak to her; there was no escaping it. And what he needed to say embarrassed him down to the buckles of his shoes. Would he be expected to speak of love? Perish the thought! He had developed a certain fondness for her quiet demeanour over the weeks of his visits, but *love*? It spoke of passion, of *frolics*. There was that word again.

'I ... um ... this is a very excellent bench, don't you think, Miss Cynthia? Sturdy yet decorative, without being at all flashy. I do so commend your mother upon her choice ...'

Cynthia murmured that her mother would be gratified to hear it.

No, that was not at all what needed to be said. He tried again.

'Have you, er, remarked upon this small tree, Miss Cynthia?

Graceful lines and it creates a very adequate screen for the woodshed.'

Cynthia quietly agreed that the woodshed would indeed be an eyesore without that convenient tree. She began to tap her foot, just a little.

'The gardener is to be congratulated,' said Pontius, becoming desperate, 'for the pleasing contrast between the red brick of the wall and the leaves of that attractive vine, don't you think?'

She didn't even deem that to be worth a response and folded her arms.

He was just wondering what on earth he *could* say, when she took his hand. That was very forward, he thought, blushing to the roots of his hat.

'Patience Pontius,' said Cynthia, looking at him intently, 'the dinner is spoiling while you are stuttering nonsense about brick walls, and Mama will be cross. What is it you wish to say to me?'

Pontius stared, his mouth opening and closing like a beached codfish. 'I ... ah ... that is ...'

'You wished to ask me to marry you, didn't you?' She squeezed his hand, and something in the curve of her lip made the word *frolics* come into his head again.

He snatched his hand away ungraciously. 'Long engagement …' he managed to spit out. 'In the fullness of time …'

'Good,' said Cynthia. 'That's settled then. We can announce it today, hmm?'

And off she went, Pontius trailing after, wondering how on earth that had happened, how she could have taken charge so utterly in a matter of moments, and still muttering, '*Very* long engagement, probably …'

The Isle of No-Such-Place

So, there he was: affianced to Miss Cynthia. Her parents had been pleased. Father Ormerod had offered congratulations. Pontius was pleased, too. He thought he was pleased. After all, this was one of the key parts of the respectable future before him. A ready-and-waiting suitable wife was a support, and it meant he was more likely to be offered a small parish to get started. They wouldn't be able to marry until something more substantial came along, and that might take, oh, years. Yes, it would certainly take years. There was plenty of time to fret about the details of marriage later on. But as time trundled on he was troubled with odd thoughts.

I know *what* I am, thought the Reverend Pontius to himself, but I'm not sure *who* I am. What he was, was a newly ordained minister in the service of the Spirit of the Sky. That was neat, and clear, and undeniable. But he remained a trifle foggy about exactly who he was. A young man with reasonable prospects, he certainly was. He had a wife organised, settled in a long engagement. He had recently been offered a little chapel, to start with. Very small it was, with no congregation to speak of, but it was an excellent opportunity to learn the trade, as it were, without doing much damage when he made the inevitable mistakes. He understood that. It was a foundation that could be built upon and progressed from in the fullness of time. He would certainly accept it. It was far too small and too ill-paid a position for a *married* minister. That was understood by all parties. He explained this to Cynthia, and she accepted it without question. He was still a very young man, and he had to start at the bottom. In time, he would be offered something more substantial. Pontius deeply hoped that might not happen too soon, though he probably wouldn't have admitted that to himself at the time. Cynthia was happy busying herself with a trousseau and a linen chest, against the day when she would need them. She made no complaints at all, and there was no more sign of her attempting to take charge of things. Pontius was grateful for all of it.

For a youngster, he wasn't especially ambitious. He didn't picture himself as a great leader, or even a small one. He would happily settle for doing a bit of good in the world, and his decision to become a minister had seemed the only respectable way to do it without being accused of having some sort of ulterior motive. His call to do good was, in fact, a great deal stronger than his wish to serve the Spirit of the Sky.

Father Ormerod had clocked this straight away. Definitely a bit lacking in the vocation department, as he'd noted at the time, but far too essentially good to turn down, not these days. Who knew? The vocation might grow on him.

So here was young Patience Pontius, fully qualified and ready to set out on his ministry. *What* he was,

was all properly organised. But, oh, he did so feel something was missing. It was something both deep and shallow, something both every-day and entirely mystical, and it was something that could show him *who* he really was, what his proper place in the world might be. But poor Pontius couldn't fathom it out.

It got lost, a bit, in the excitement of taking on the little chapel, of being a new broom sweeping clean and trying to get the hole in the roof fixed. It got buried under the pile of books when the Reverend tried his hand at sermon-writing and created sermons so obscure that even the most devout members of the tiny congregation couldn't keep their eyes open. It fell to the bottom of his basket of comforts when he went on his rounds of the sick and needy. But that "Who-am-I?" question never truly left him, never was answered, and was always ready to ambush him in the small hours of the night. It annoyed him a great deal.

As is so often the case, the solution did not appear to Pontius in a blinding revelation. How simple and satisfying that would have been. But no, it crept up on him in a downright sneaky way, when he wasn't looking. And it was wearing an impenetrable disguise, to boot. Enough to confuse anybody. The young Pontius was about to discover that who he was, was not at all what he had expected. And it began, a few weeks later, in a most singular manner.

In the beginning, there was a list. It was a list of things to do, of the kind that any busy individual might scribble down so that nothing should be forgotten. Pontius was emptying his pockets one evening, clearing out loose change. It did so wear out the linings. There were a couple of keys, too, equally damaging to the pockets. A mint humbug, slightly fluffy. A handkerchief that was long overdue for laundering. And a list, folded in four. Probably an old one, Pontius thought, tutting to himself, but it was as well to make sure.

He took it over to the candle and squinted at it. Oh, yes. He had made this list, oh, a couple of weeks ago. He let his eye run down it:

Item, church flowers, enquire re. That's done.

Item, thatch v slate for church roof, which best? Slate too expensive, so that's settled, too.

Item, collect cheese. It had been far too mouldy, and he'd had a tiff with the dairyman.

Item, Larus, Isle of, enquire re. What?

Pontius stared. He hadn't written that, had he? He was sure he hadn't. But it was undoubtedly in his own hand. Had he misread it, misconstrued his own writing? No. It was entirely clear. He frowned. It made no sense at all. Larus? He'd never heard of it. How could he have made a note of something he'd never heard of? Not only that, but he lived a long way inland. Islands were pretty thin on the ground in these parts. Even if it had actually slipped his mind, which he was sure it hadn't, what possible interest could he have had in such a place? It was most perplexing. He could only think it was something he'd overheard and made a note to investigate. But he had no recollection of doing any such thing.

'Well,' he said to himself, 'I must have thought it interesting at the time, I suppose.' And he resolved to ask Father Ormerod if he could shed light on the mystery when next they met.

'No such place,' said Father Ormerod, sniffily, when Pontius asked about the Isle of Larus. 'It is fabulous. I mean it's a fable. Not real. Non-existent.'

That seemed an excessive number of denials. 'Are you sure?' That was a foolish question, and impertinent, but he pressed on. 'My, um, informant was quite clear on the matter.' Pontius thought it best not to add that said informant was himself, and that he had no recollection of how he had heard of it.

'My son, there is no such place.'

'Then how do you know about it?' Pontius was aware he was pushing his luck to the limit, possibly indulging in disrespect for his mentor, and steadied himself for an earful. Father Ormerod could be quite forceful when he was annoyed, and annoyed he clearly was.

'Listen very carefully, young man, I shall not say this again. Larus is a chimera, a whimsy, a mere illusion. People tell stories about it, but that doesn't mean it's real. It is a fairy tale.'

'But I never heard of it before,' protested Pontius.

'That, young man, is because you have thus far moved in the right circles, including and especially mine. The ministry of the Spirit of the Sky does not indulge in fairy tales about non-existent things. I recommend you bear that in mind and speak no more of this. Ever.'

'I was ... simply seeking guidance, Father,' said Pontius, apologetically, though he couldn't for the life of him see what he had to apologise for.

'And guidance you have had,' said Father Ormerod, looking so closely at Pontius that he felt his heart and mind had been pierced. 'The matter is closed.'

That was very final, and Pontius bowed his head in defeat. But he had no intention at all of letting the matter drop. Father Ormerod was clearly not the best person to ask. He had no idea why his mentor should be so annoyed about a query regarding a place that apparently didn't exist. Pontius had never in his life disobeyed, least of all disobeyed Father Ormerod, but he felt compelled to get to the bottom of it. It was simply a matter of some gentle detective work, wasn't it? Of asking the right questions in the right places? Somewhere deep down, the young Reverend Pontius felt a thrill of anticipation. Not only that; he knew just the right place to begin his clandestine enquiries. But the idea made him queasy. The question was not whether he could, but whether he should. Was it important enough, truly, to risk a breach with Father Ormerod?

The Words on the Window

Pontius trudged back to his lodgings that evening and slumped on the bed, confused and weary. The little chapel didn't merit its own accommodations, and it was a fair walk to and fro. Unless he was otherwise engaged, he tended to stay at the church all day. He sometimes wondered whether he might find a corner to sleep in and be done with it. He wasn't the sort of young man to worry excessively about his surroundings, and it might even improve security a little. Things did tend to go missing when they were unattended. This was probably not allowed, he guessed, and he wasn't about to annoy Father Ormerod by making any further unconventional requests. So, he persisted in his gloomy lodgings with the bed that seemed always slightly damp, and the inadequate light from the small window.

He was supposed to be writing a sermon, so he unpacked a sheet of paper from a bundle marked "sermons, for the writing of", and tried to apply himself to that dull task. But he didn't make much progress and he found he had spoiled the paper by thoughtlessly writing

"Isle of Larus, enquire re" instead of anything at all sermon-like.

'Perhaps,' he murmured, 'perhaps I am simply wrong; simply pursuing a fairy-tale.' It was stubborn and pig-headed to continue with this little quest, and it annoyed the college, most specifically Father Ormerod. Not a very good start to his ministry, was it? And all for a bit of frolicsome nonsense. After all, if he did succeed in solving the mystery of the Isle of Larus, what exactly would he do with that knowledge, eh? Pontius couldn't answer that question. What was it all for, beyond satisfying his curiosity? It was surely the worst kind of self-indulgence. He was still only a very junior minister, and he was getting up the noses of his superiors, maybe even jeopardising his future before it had even begun, and all for asking questions. Both the college and Father Ormerod might turn out to have limited patience, and the next nice placing, the next rung on the ladder for his career, could be handed to someone who was prepared to be less nosy and to take no for an answer.

He thought mournfully of Cynthia (he always seemed to think of her mournfully nowadays). Whatever would she say if she knew he was taking such a risk with his future? With *their* future? There is nothing else for it, Pontius thought, as he put on his nightcap against the chill; I must give up this nonsense, forget it. Starting this minute.

He awoke feeling refreshed, relieved, rejuvenated. His little bit of madness was over, ready to be filed away under the heading of foolish nonsense and damn silly ideas, pardon the language. Pontius got up and fairly skipped over to the window to pull aside the dark and dusty drapes and let some light into the world. 'Oh!' he said.

Clearly written in the condensation on the window glass were the words *Larus ha ha.* Pontius jumped back, startled. It wasn't just the message; he would deal with that in a moment. One thing at a time please. The disturbing thing was that they were written on the inside: that they could only mean someone had been in the room. Someone with worrying knowledge of the matter that had bothered him night and day. Pontius tore his eyes away from the window and went to try the door. Locked. And bolted. How could anybody have got in? And who exactly would wish to, just to write on the windowpane? The only person he had spoken to about all this was Father Ormerod, and his reaction had been pretty hostile, all things considered. So why would he want to stir up Pontius' curiosity again? And that was without any consideration of how he might have got through a locked door to do it without making an almighty racket.

'Another mystery,' said Pontius to himself, and watched as the condensation began to run and the words began to vanish. 'Though how I shall solve it I don't know.' All his resolutions and good intentions of the night before trickled away with the water.

He took a sheet of paper, sermons for the writing of, and wrote instead *Larus ha ha*, as if he were likely to forget it, and then looked guiltily around as if Father Ormerod might materialise and tell him that not only was is a forbidden subject but also a frightful waste of expensive paper.

What could it mean, *Larus ha ha*? It didn't make much sense. Pontius couldn't help thinking it was another connection with the word *frolic* that seemed to follow him in a recurring way. The written laugh, ha ha, was a frolicsome thing, wasn't it? He imagined so. To be honest, Pontius was not a man with much of a sense of humour and, for that matter, Father Ormerod had taken a turn for the humourless lately. Surely, he could not be responsible for this odd turn of events? But if not him, then who had done it, and how?

But Pontius was not to be stopped this time. Words written on his own window, by a hand unknown, whoever it was, had made the whole thing *personal*—not simply a matter of idle curiosity. The latent detective in his soul stirred again and said, 'We shall have to be more methodical about this. And a bit more secretive, too. And never mind what Father Ormerod thinks. What he doesn't know won't harm him, will it?' Pontius wasn't sure if what he was about to do was harm-free, exactly, but he was determined to find out what was going on. 'At any cost?' asked his inner detective. Yes. At any cost.

The best place to start was with a bit of research at the college library. It was a little dangerous, perhaps, but Pontius couldn't help a thrill of anticipation, at the sheer naughtiness of doing something that would certainly be frowned upon. And might have severe consequences for his future. Pontius had never thought of himself of a risk-taker, and here he was setting out on a very risky path. His heart raced with delicious delight at the thought of it.

The Merry Isle

Pontius had been aghast at the reception his question about the Isle of Larus had had from Father Ormerod. Clearly he would receive no help from that quarter, though he was entirely puzzled at the vehement response. Why would his mentor take so violent an opposition to a place he didn't believe existed? If it were truly just a fairy tale, then why all the foot-stamping and shouting? Father Ormerod was generally so even-tempered, too. It didn't add up and Pontius was at a loss. But it did arouse in him a stubborn streak he hadn't known he possessed.

So, what was it about Larus, real or not, that could so upset a perfectly sensible senior man of the cloth? The answer presumably lay in the details of the legend. So, Pontius began his investigations in the college library. It wasn't a very extensive book collection; they were expensive objects, after all, but it seemed a good place to begin.

I shall avoid the librarian if I can, Pontius told himself, or if he insists on knowing my purpose, I'll say ... What could he say? Not that he was seeking information on the Isle of Larus. Father Ormerod had already made it clear this was a forbidden subject, and even mentioning it to the librarian could have unhappy consequences. He could say he was doing some general reading to broaden his knowledge. It wasn't exactly true, but not exactly untrue either. He simply wanted to broaden his knowledge in a Larus-ward direction.

It may have been only a small library, but there were a great many pages in the books. Pontius scanned them till his eyes ached with weariness, and at last was ejected by the librarian, who wanted his dinner and needed to lock the place up. When Pontius offered to lock up after himself and drop off the keys later, the librarian said it was more than his job was worth, that the library would be open again tomorrow, and hustled him briskly outside.

Am I wasting my time on this, Pontius wondered? There were still an awful lot of books to look through. And it was possible his repeated presence might be reported to Father Ormerod, who might put two and two together and guess what he was up to. So, he left it a few days before returning and continuing his reading, keeping as quiet as possible, and restricting the time he spent in the library. He hoped that would look a little less suspicious.

On this third return to the library, the librarian had glared at him, and Pontius began to fear he would be barred for time-wasting. He had also begun to peer guiltily over his shoulder, in case Father Ormerod should burst in and demand to know why he was there. It was all very stressful, and he hadn't found a single mention of the Isle of Larus, not anywhere. This will be the last book I consult, he thought, opening a musty volume, and then I'll give it up. As the thought crossed his mind, his eye fell on a page unhappily titled "Unpermitted". He knew just how it felt and looked idly down the list of unpermitted things. And then he saw it. Under a dismal subsection entitled "Especially Unpermitted" there lay a single entry: "The Merry Isle", it said, "To Be Avoided".

'The Merry Isle?' murmured Pontius. 'I wish it could be more specific.'

'Well, *I* can be specific,' said a voice by his ear. Pontius nearly jumped out of his skin. The librarian had crept up behind him and was looking over his shoulder. 'You never said anything about looking up unpermitted things. Out, and don't come back!'

'I ... but, I didn't know,' Pontius said truthfully, as he was taken by the scruff of the neck. The librarian was surprisingly strong for someone who had spent a lifetime immersed in books. Pontius stammered and apologised, though he didn't really know what to apologise for, all the way to the door, and found himself thrown out once and for all. It was true he'd been a little underhanded, of necessity, about what he was looking for, but it had never occurred to him it might be entirely unpermitted.

'I have been naïve,' he said to himself, as he brushed down his coat and polished his shoe buckle on the back of his stocking to remove the mark left when the librarian had trodden on his foot on the way out. But, oh, it didn't matter. The library had finally furnished him with a clue. Could the "Merry Isle, To Be Avoided", possibly be the Isle of Larus? It would at least explain Father Ormerod's reaction to his questions, if he had been enquiring about unpermitted things, though it would have been more helpful if he'd simply said so. Pontius had the strong feeling he was on the right track. But the solution to one question had clearly thrown up another: what exactly was wrong with the Merry Isle, or Larus, if that was indeed its true name? And how on earth could he hope to find out?

❧

There was no doubt about it, Father Ormerod had changed. But he hadn't improved. It seemed only five minutes ago he had jovially suggested to Pontius that a bit of frolicking might be in order. And now, well, the annoying twinkles that had once sparkled in his eyes were gone; shadows fell over his face whenever they met and frolicking never got a mention at all.

Pontius couldn't make it out. It wasn't just the sudden change in his mentor's demeanour, it was the difficulty of working out why that change had occurred. He knew, to the hour, *when* it had occurred; it was the moment he had mentioned the Isle of Larus that the shutters had come down. They were showing no signs of coming up again, either. Pontius had been careful to say nothing, to give every indication of having forgotten all about it. But still the dark looks continued. Father Ormerod had been the nearest thing to a friend that Pontius had, and he missed that relaxed relationship very much. He wasn't the sort of young fellow who made friends so very easily.

It's not me who's acting irrationally, Pontius thought, crossly. It's not me who's refusing point-blank to discuss things and being all mysterious about it. It's not me who's being so touchy.

However, said his inner voice, it is *me* that's planning to go on investigating this mad Larus thing, despite being expressly forbidden; I suppose, in the end, that makes us about even.

The Know-It-All Inn

'Hello dearie,' said a soft female voice close by his ear. Pontius jumped. He hadn't seen her in the shadows. Well, to be honest, he hadn't been paying full attention.

'Can I do something for you?'

'Ah,' said Pontius, still not paying full attention, 'perhaps you can.' He felt in his pocket for a coin. Information never seemed to come free of charge.

The woman stepped out into the meagre moonlight. It was enough for him to become aware of the shocking disarray of her dress. Why, she was almost falling out of it. To his horror and mortification, Pontius realised he was being offered frolics of a quite different kind.

In his haste to put distance between them, he stepped back so suddenly he nearly fell in a puddle.

'Careful, dearie,' she said, smirking. 'Wouldn' want t' spoil your fine clothes, would ye? Now then, I can give you a very 'appy time at a very reas'nable price. What d'you say?'

'Madam,' said Pontius, now paying good attention, 'how dare you? I'm a ...' He was about to say, "a man of the cloth", but caught himself just in time. Supposing word got back that a minister of the church, dressed in non-clerical clothing, had been seen lurking about the unsavoury end of town, talking about unseemly matters to, er, ladies to whom he had not been formally introduced? Suppose Father Ormerod found out? Suppose Cynthia found out? I am teetering on the brink of disaster, he thought.

'You're a what, dearie?' said the woman, who looked as if nothing he might say would surprise her.

Pontius pulled himself upright, got his mind together and improvised. 'I'm a-looking for information. The Know-it-All Inn. Can you direct me to it if you please?'

'I can,' she said. 'Just down at the end o' the street. Shall I come with you?'

'No,' said Pontius, backing off yet again and putting one foot squarely in the filthy puddle. 'No, that will not be necessary. Here, take this for your trouble, madam. I thank you kindly.'

And he squelched off down the street, unable to resist turning to see if she might be following. But thankfully she had vanished back into the shadows.

It had been a very bad idea, he decided, to come to this place, the scruffy and disreputable end of the town, and his first instinct was to scurry home before anything worse could happen. It had seemed only too logical, just an hour or so earlier, to put on some old clothes—the very clothes in which he had arrived at the theological college—and which had lurked in the back of a cupboard ever since, and head for somewhere he might hope to meet ordinary folks. Ordinary folks, he hoped, that might be less unwilling to talk about the Isle of Larus or the Merry Isle, or both, if they should prove to be one and the same. He had heard his fellow students speak of the Know-it-All Inn. They had chuckled awkwardly and nudged each other's elbows and shut up like clams when Father Ormerod approached. It was the only disreputable place Pontius had ever heard mentioned, so naturally it was his first port of call. But oh, the discomfort! Not only were his old clothes now on the tight side, the waistcoat buttons threatening to go their own ways, but he was aware of his own naivety. The college had not prepared him for ordinary folks, for people who didn't necessarily obey the rules of polite society. I suppose I will need to learn, he thought, and this is as good a place to begin as any. So, despite misgivings, he went blundering into the Know-it-All Inn, sincerely hoping that it might live up to its name.

*

'The Merry Isle, is it?'
The man looked at Pontius so intently that he immediately felt so guilty he was tempted to blurt out, 'Don't tell Father Ormerod.'

'You've heard tell of it, then, have you?' Pontius asked, as casually as he could manage.

The man looked pointedly at Pontius, and then at his empty tankard, 'Maybe.'

'Ah, er, perhaps I could refill that for you.' Pontius was a little slow on the uptake.

'Aye, you could.'

Pontius called for more ale, and awaited developments.

'Well, now. The Merry Isle.' The man looked Pontius up and down. 'Seems to me you're a man o' the cloth, sir.'

How the devil did he know that? And after all that trouble with his clothing, too. 'What if I am?' said Pontius defensively, and then realised he'd probably given himself away.

'Odd sort o' question for a man o' the cloth.'

Pontius gave in. 'Yes, I know. It's unpermitted. What can you tell me?' He wondered how much information a tankard of ale might be worth.

The man chuckled. 'Well, now, the thing you need to know about the Merry Isle is …'

Pontius' ear picked out the word "Larus" from a conversation at the adjoining table. Had they been listening in? Did this mean the Merry Isle and Larus were one and the same? Or was it pure coincidence?

But his informant was continuing, and Pontius was trying to listen to two conversations at once. 'The thing about the Merry Isle is that it isn't really the isle what's merry.'

'Eh?' said Pontius. What on earth was that supposed to mean? He opened his mouth to demand an explanation but stopped dead. Father Ormerod had just walked into the tavern.

'Men o' the cloth,' said his informant, noting that Pontius had vanished under the table, 'Y' never know what they'll do next. Hee, hee.'

Had he been seen? Had Father Ormerod followed him? Or was it just another odd coincidence? The questions crowded Pontius' mind as he cowered under the table. His heart pounded with terror at being caught in such a situation, and he waited for Father Ormerod's thunder-cloud face to appear between the table legs. The minutes passed, and he became aware of cramp in his foot and cobwebs in his hair from the underside of the table; his left knee had landed in something damp and sticky. But there was still no sign of a wrathful Father Ormerod. Drips of spilt ale fell off the tabletop and onto Pontius' shoulder. He tried to identify his mentor's feet among all the others but couldn't find them. It struck him as odd that the place hadn't fallen silent at the sudden arrival of a clergyman. The chatter and laughter continued as before. Strange. Did this mean Father Ormerod's arrival was nothing out of the ordinary? Pontius boggled at the thought. How could that be? He would deal with that interesting question later but, for now, how on earth was he to get out of the place unobserved? He had been under the table, oh, hours and hours it seemed, when a voice said, 'You can come out now, young feller. He's gone.'

Pontius emerged cautiously, brushing himself down as best he could. His stockings were blotted with greasy stains, and as he pulled himself back onto the bench the buttons of his waistcoat finally gave up the unequal struggle and burst open, one of them actually pulling itself off its moorings and skittering across the table.

The man he had been speaking to was still there, wearing a very knowing grin. 'Thought y' was a man o' the cloth. Is this yours?' And he handed back the button.

'Thank you,' said Pontius, desperately trying to gather some shred of dignity. He was desperate to leave the place, but would he find Father Ormerod lurking outside, ready to pounce?

'Best way is out the back door,' said the man, as if he assisted clergymen to escape low taverns on a regular basis. 'No one'll see you. Best keep a hold on your purse, though.'

Pontius fled.

A Tempting Offer

It was much later, when Pontius crept shame-faced back to his lodgings, doing his best to conceal his grubby clothes from prying eyes, that he thought through what had been said. Not much, in truth. It had just been getting interesting when Father Ormerod's arrival had spoiled it. Something about the Merry Isle not being the thing that was merry. Very cryptic. So, something else was merry, then. But what? And that overheard conversation with the clear word "Larus". Or had he imagined it, heard what he so wanted to hear? If it had been real, could it have been pure coincidence? There was far too much coincidence going on for Pontius to dismiss it, and he occupied himself with writing down everything he could remember that had been said. There was also the matter of what Father Ormerod had been doing in such a place. Did he follow me? Or does he go there on a regular basis? Both possibilities threw up some very worrying questions. Perhaps the other students, the ones who had mentioned the place with a snigger, sneaked down to that tavern and now and then, and Father Ormerod was in the habit of following them. If he had, indeed, followed Pontius, the game was up. He couldn't help thinking that Father Ormerod was in possession of a very suspicious mind. All in all, Pontius thought, I have really made no progress at all, and I dare not risk going back.

'You have been seen in some low establishments, mixing with low people.' Father Ormerod came straight to the point.

Pontius was tempted to observe that Father Ormerod knocked about in some pretty low establishments himself and, what's more, appeared to be entirely at ease in them. But this was not the moment for impertinent rejoinders.

'What have you to say for yourself?'

Pontius stuttered. What exactly *had* he got to say for himself? 'It's my duty to know the people hereabouts, all of them,' he said defensively. 'Good works ... poor and needy ... suitable, um, sermons ...' he trailed off.

'My boy,' said Father Ormerod, sounding more like his old self, at least for a moment, 'perhaps you have been working too hard.' He placed a fatherly hand on Pontius' shoulder and went on, 'Take your time. You have a good heart, which is the main thing you need. You have it in you to become a very adequate minister. But these wild questions and claims you have indulged in will do you no good at all.'

Pontius winced, waiting. Father Ormerod looked him squarely in the eye. 'So, let's have no more of this. I can tell you in confidence that a very pleasant living with an attractive church and an attentive congregation is shortly to become vacant. I could put your name forward, you know. I have a *little* influence.' His eyes twinkled in the old way. 'You could marry your young lady—there will be an increase in stipend—and set yourself up very nicely, with excellent future prospects. So, think about it, young Pontius, and give me your decision. You have a month.'

And with that, Father Ormerod swept out, pausing in the doorway only long enough to say, 'And if I catch you in a low tavern again, I'll have the hide off you. Do you understand?'

Pontius goggled, not for the first time. He had just been given the best offer a young man could hope for: an assured future, a dutiful wife, and a decent congregation thrown in.

So why did he find himself hesitating? He could run after Father Ormerod and say that he didn't need a month, or even a minute. He would take it, yes please. It was likely Father Ormerod was expecting just that outcome, and that taking the full month wouldn't stand in Pontius' favour.

So, he lived up to expectations, dashed out and caught up with his mentor. 'Father Ormerod,' he said earnestly, 'I shall speak to my fiancée when I go to dinner with her parents next week.'

Father Ormerod gave a satisfied nod and walked away.

The Spirit of the Sea

It worried young Pontius very deeply that although he was committed to the Spirit of the Sky, the deity had never directly spoken to him, offered him clear guidance, or, indeed, truly indicated that he was doing the right thing. He had always put this down to the Spirit being merely a taciturn type, or perhaps too busy to be dealing with such a very low-ranking clergyman as himself. Pontius had always been wary of curiosity and didn't like to ask the real reason for this state of affairs. So, it came as a surprise to him when insight, of a sort, was granted out of the blue, only a day or so after the confrontation with Father Ormerod.

It came down to that weasel-word *frolic* again, which had troubled him so often. And that other weasel-word *merry,* which now troubled him too. He was running a duster over his pews one morning and thinking aloud. 'I can't believe the Spirit of the Sky would approve of frolics,' he said to himself. 'It just doesn't seem fitting.'

'I should think not!' said a voice close by his elbow. Pontius nearly jumped out of his skin.

'Who's there? Come out at once, I have a sword!' yelled Pontius, without thinking that was a rash claim to make for someone armed only with a duster.

'No need for that, your reverendness! No harm meant, I'm sure.' A man straightened up, having apparently been resting under a pew. 'Sorry if I startled you, but it was what you was saying, sir.'

Pontius reassembled his scattered wits and thought a moment, frowning. What was it I said? Oh, yes, *frolics.*

'Regarding frolics, sir, if that's what you's a-wanting, well that would be more in the line of the Spirit of the Sea, you see. Your spirit, the Spirit of the Sky, is more of a dour sort. Oh yes, indeed.'

'The Spirit of the *Sea*?' It was the first Pontius had heard of any such entity and it threw him into confusion. 'Eh?'

'I see this is a new idea t' ye, young sir,' said the man, stretching his arms and yawning. 'Not much heard of, this far inland, I dare say. But I have travelled, sir, seen the sea, and ridden on it too, and I can assure you the Spirit of the Sea is entirely real—has a superb sense of humour, quite a prankster, too. And would most certainly be interested in any sort of frolicsomeness.'

Pontius was still reeling from the revelation that there might be a second deity to deal with. He found one quite enough to be going on with. Father Ormerod had never said anything about this. Through all the days of his studies, no one at all had ever suggested there might be multiple deities. Why not? Was this scruffy fellow being untruthful, passing the time of day by trying to dupe a man of the cloth? Or was it genuine? Had he been deceived all this time? Pontius had the presence of mind to decide that he had better check it out before he went galloping off to Father

Ormerod, demanding explanations. 'I've never heard of it,' he said carefully, which was true, but didn't openly accuse the chap of lying.

'Ye've never left this part of the world, have ye?' said the man, with a knowing look. Pontius shook his head. It was true.

'The people who get their livings from the sea: fisherfolk, and sea-going types, they worship the Spirit of the Sea. And I doubt they'd have any truck with your Spirit of the Sky, though I guess they might have heard of it. The sea means everything to 'em, y'see. No use for sky-born spirits, not really.'

'No use for the Spirit of the Sky?' spluttered Pontius in indignation. 'That's ...' he searched for the right word. What was that word Father Ormerod used for ridiculous things? Oh, yes, 'Preposterous!'

'True though,' said the man, chuckling.

How dare the fellow chuckle at such a thing! Pontius closed his eyes a moment, gathering all the righteous indignation he could muster. 'I protest ...'

But the man had gone. Pontius turned a full circle, looking. He even peered under the pew. But there wasn't a sign of the fellow. Might have just evaporated into thin air—*pop*! Except that was impossible.

Pontius stood a moment, trying to sort through what had just happened. Could it be true? Could he have been kept in the dark all this time? Could everything he'd sincerely accepted and believed be wrong? And what was the connection with the Isle of Larus, if there was one? The only obvious connection was the sea. A wee bit tenuous.

Poor Pontius. He now had two mysteries to deal with: the question of Larus, real or not, was one thing but the possibility of a whole other deity to deal with was far more serious. And alarming, too. He broke out into a sweat and absent-mindedly mopped his brow with the duster.

Paved with Pearls

Pontius felt his once-good relationship with Father Ormerod had gone from bad to impossible.

And as for the matter of the mysterious Spirit of the Sea, well, it clearly wasn't safe to go enquiring after alternative deities, however much the subject might be on his mind. He honestly didn't know whether it was actually a bad thing or not. If he stretched his mind a wee bit, he could accept that people in different places might have different needs in terms of deities. Or even, perhaps, have no need of them at all. But it was a tricky subject, however you might approach it.

The best he could do was to consider the Spirit of the Sea as a local legend. An old god, perhaps long-forgotten. Surely, then, it was not a rival of the Spirit of the Sky in any meaningful way, which was why neither Father Ormerod nor anybody else had ever mentioned it. Still, he shuddered to think of his mentor's reaction to any casual questioning on the subject. What he did know, absolutely and finally, was that he had to solve these multiple mysteries, sort them out good and proper, and go forward with his eyes fully open if he were to have any future as a minister. And he was equally sure that he wouldn't be finding the answers he needed locally. He would have to go and *look* for them. And the place to find the answers was the sea. But, oh, a whole raft of difficulties was towed behind *that* idea.

He and Cynthia had braved the winter weather, muffled in warm cloaks. Out in the snowy garden, or in several degrees of frost, the fortnightly tete-a-tete continued, more out of habit than any desire on Pontius' part. He had told her about his interest in the Isle of Larus, despite it being an "unpermitted" subject. Their conversations had gone round in circles.

'Why is it unpermitted, Patience?'

'I do not know.'

'Can you not ask Father Ormerod?'

'He has forbidden me to mention it.' Pontius neglected to add how upset and annoyed, and distant Father Ormerod had become.

'Can you not find out by some other means?'

'I have been forbidden to use the library for that purpose.' Thrown out, actually, but he hadn't mentioned that either. As to being caught asking questions in a low tavern ... Well, he was certainly not going to say anything about that regrettable episode, not least because it might lead back to the woman of the night he had spoken to.

'Then should you not give up your pursuit of it?'

'I suppose I should,' Suppose? There was no suppose about it—of course, he should. But would he do so? No, he would not. 'But I feel I need to know.'

Cynthia looked perplexed, but not as disapproving as Pontius might have expected. He thought he understood her thoughts: she respected his need to know but was concerned about any defiance of Father Ormerod. That would be natural enough. Her parents would certainly be concerned if they knew, and she was a dutiful daughter. And yet, Pontius thought, there was something in her manner that was strangely supportive. He couldn't quite make it out. She had certainly not refused to discuss the matter.

'Tell me again,' she would say, seriously.

'Well, it's an imaginary, that is to say, er legendary island, which probably doesn't exist. But might do.' It sounded so feeble. Pontius had not felt able to confide in her regarding the words that had appeared so mysteriously on his bedroom window, the words written in the dust of the pew, or the man who had said interesting things then so promptly disappeared. She would think him deranged. And what her parents would say, if she passed such information on, didn't bear thinking about. Not only that, but it would also all get back to Father Ormerod and that wouldn't do at all.

So, Pontius spoke only of the fabulous isle, describing it as a tiny jewel set in a silver sea, peopled by kind-hearted individuals. A little earthly paradise, entirely of his own invention. He said nothing about actually going to look for it; he hoped she would understand that this was his ultimate aim without the need to say so out loud and in detail. Cynthia listened enraptured and in silence, week by week, as Pontius embroidered the tale as far as his limited imagination would take it. Would sheep with golden fleeces be taking it too far? How about roads paved with pearls? Cliffs made of solid- silver? At no point did she tell him any of it was beyond belief.

For all these conversations, which he hoped might prepare the way, he had put off the final one, more than once. But the spring was coming in, time was running out and now it had to be done. Today.

She had greeted him with smiles. Pontius had fervently hoped she would have anticipated his words, that women's intuition would have told her what he had to say. But no. All smiles, each one entering his heart like a dagger.

They sat in her parents' garden, as so many times before. The snow had gone, and it was cherry blossom that fluttered around them now. Cynthia had bits of blossom in her hair, making her look just like a bride. Pontius turned words and phrases over in his head, rejecting them all as not good enough, not clear enough. Cynthia said nothing, waiting with her hands crossed modestly in her lap, but with a secret smile of understanding. Pontius was horrified. She had anticipated it; her women's intuition had told her. And it had told her entirely the wrong thing.

'You are very quiet, Patience,' she said at last, still smiling.

'I ... um ... I ... That is ...' he babbled, blushing. She smiled encouragingly again at his confusion. She misunderstands me, he thought, in despair. And then with sudden, awful clarity, he realised what she was expecting. She thinks I shall ask her to set the wedding day! And that we shall announce it to her mother and father over dinner, too. She expects to go indoors as a soon-to-be bride. She has misunderstood everything I have said. All my thoughts of distant travel, my searches after the truth, however much dressed up in roads paved with pearls and whatnot. *She expects to go with me.* I have not made it clear that I need to do this alone, that a wife is not part of the plan.

She was still smiling, anticipating the happiest of outcomes.

'You know I care very much for you, Patience,' she said. More gentle encouragement. How was he to tell her the truth, shoot her down, like a soaring dove transfixed by an arrow? There was no way to do it without causing pain and humiliation of the worst kind for a young woman who was expecting to be made entirely happy.

'My mother says it has been a long enough engagement,' she added gravely. Now it was Pontius who felt transfixed by the blasted arrow. How, how, could he find a way out of this?

'Miss Cynthia,' he said, as formally as he could, edging surreptitiously towards the far end of the bench, 'I fear you have …'

But that was as far as he could get. Cynthia's mother was at the garden door, cheerfully calling them in to dinner.

He stood up quickly, automatically offering her his arm. She took it, but not before glancing up into his face. Pontius saw that she had understood, put two and two together at last. Her smile was destroyed, tears gathering, and a flush of deepest embarrassment was making its splashy way across her face. There was no need for him to say anything else. Their engagement was at an end; he didn't know whether to be relieved or mortified.

'I'm so sorry,' he murmured, knowing those words simply twisted the knife. There would be pity enough for her to endure.

Cynthia took a shuddering breath, but said nothing, and set off on her way indoors, dragging him with her. The meal about to be served would be a very uncomfortable occasion indeed.

Oh, uncomfortable hadn't been the half of it. Cynthia had held herself together with remarkable fortitude, making polite small talk throughout the meal. Meaningful looks had been exchanged between her parents, between Cynthia and her mother, and among all three of them. It must have been torture for her, Pontius thought ruefully; it had certainly been so for him.

When he left, as soon as was politely possible, she escorted him to the garden gate, and there reached the end of her strength. The tears flowed; Pontius offered her his handkerchief, helplessly mumbling apologies and saying it was probably all for the best, though he was sure she couldn't possibly agree. There wasn't much that could happen in the life of a well-bred young woman that was worse than being jilted, now was there?

How could he lessen the blow? Pontius had an idea, though he was unsure if it were a good one. 'Please tell people, if you wish, that it was you that broke off our engagement—that you found me unsuitable. Too flighty.

Unreliable. Not ideal husband material.'

She stared at him. '*Flighty*? You, Patience?'

He felt he was digging himself into a very deep hole. 'Well, Father Ormerod says I'm chasing an impossibility in seeking out that island, that Larus, which may not be real at all. That's flighty, isn't it?'

'But the sheep with fleeces of gold, the roads paved with pearls?'

'I made them up,' said Pontius, hopelessly. 'I don't know if there's anything there at all.'

'So, I'm losing you to a non-existent place, is that it?'

It sounded so ridiculous that Pontius was silenced. It wasn't entirely true, either. In a sense, the seeking out of the Isle of Larus was an excuse, and a fairly flimsy one, for the fact that marriage to a modest and sensible girl like Cynthia, one who in theory suited him perfectly, simply was no longer a very appealing future. He had suffered a degree of infatuation for her, to begin with, but that had long since faded. He wanted something more, though he hardly knew what. The mysterious Isle of Larus had stepped into the breach and filled his head with longing for the unknown. As for his queries regarding this ostensible Spirit of the Sea, he certainly couldn't mention them, for fear of adding impropriety to madness. So, he had left that subject untouched.

Later, Pontius wondered if she had regretted losing him as much as losing the possibility of a respectable marriage. Or was it the possibility of accompanying him to the impossible place he had described that had appealed to her? Were her tears for him, for their lost respectable future, or for the end of an adventurous dream she had entertained? He convinced himself it was the respectable future she wept for; it was, at least, a way to allow himself to feel a little less villainous, to feel less like a trifler with female affections. She would find another man to marry, perhaps; Pontius comforted himself with the thought that if all she truly wanted was a respectable marriage, there would be other opportunities for her. He had already allowed her the opportunity to say in public that she had found him unsuitable—that it had been her choice.

Still, it made him shudder to think of the final scene: he had left Cynthia crying at the gate of that beautiful little garden, swathed in falling cherry blossom. There was no excusing that; he had wounded her deeply, whatever her motives. Destroyed her hopes; it was a dastardly deed for a so-called gentleman, and a man of the cloth to boot.

The words went round and round his head: *I left her crying in the garden.* They haunted him for a long while.

Vocation, Vocation, and, er, Vocation

'It is a leap of faith,' said Pontius earnestly; to be honest, he wasn't sure whether it was a leap of faith or a jump off a cliff.

Father Ormerod, judging by his expression, clearly shared that doubt. He turned and began to stroll ponderously down the aisle of the little church, with Pontius trailing behind muttering, 'Do mind the loose flagstones, if you please; people have fallen …' He didn't want his mentor to go sprawling, however much of a welcome distraction that might provide to the tension of the moment.

'You are throwing away your future,' said Father Ormerod over his shoulder. Pontius had anticipated this reaction a million times and couldn't quite prevent himself from rolling his eyes and mouthing the words. There was nothing he could say in his defence.

'A leap of faith,' said Father Ormerod. 'It is something all of us in the ministry of the Spirit of the Sky must sometimes make.' He made it sound eminently reasonable; it *was* eminently reasonable. 'But what you say makes no sense at all.'

Pontius knew that. He had tried so hard to explain, to put his case. He had told Father Ormerod that he had never experienced a vocation, a calling, from the Spirit of the Sky. Father Ormerod had answered that it was natural to have one's doubts, that everyone did at times, which was where the leap of faith came in.

'Father, you don't understand,' Pontius had begged. He tried to find the words. The calling had been loud and clear, but it had been from the Isle of Larus, real or unreal.

'You can't have a vocation from a *mythical place*,' Father Ormerod had snapped. 'That's nonsense.'

'Then perhaps,' Pontius had faltered, 'it came from the Spirit of the Sea.'

Father Ormerod had been rendered speechless at that one, or at least for as long as it took him to build up a bit of steam. 'Let me make myself perfectly clear.' Pontius had no doubt that his mentor was about to do just that. 'There is no such thing as the Spirit of the Sea. You cannot receive a vocation from a non-existent spirit any more than you can receive one from your ridiculous imaginary island. Do you understand?' Pontius did, of course, but the fact remained that the compulsion he felt to find Larus had taken root in his heart, and it was outweighing everything, including the thunderous look on his mentor's face.

'Larus is real,' he said stoutly, 'I know it and it calls me. It is a leap of faith, and it's one I must take. As to the Spirit of the Sea ...' He trailed off; this was something he was far less certain about. Spirits were supposed to be serious-minded, responsible: it was what he had always understood and here was a spirit with the heart of a prankster, apparently. It was an alarming idea, and one that made him uncomfortable. And yet he felt its presence. In his wilder moments, Pontius could almost have thought it was the Spirit of the Sea that had put the word *frolics* into Father Ormerod's mouth all those months ago. That would explain a great deal; everything, in fact, except why the Spirit of the Sea would want him to find the Isle of Larus. Assuming they actually existed, which was still open to considerable doubt. What would either of them want with him?

'So, you are abandoning the Spirit of the Sky for these imaginary things?' asked Father Ormerod, frowning. The disbelief in his voice made Pontius squirm in his shoes. Put like that …

'Oh no,' he said at once. 'Never; I shall always be the servant of the Spirit of the Sky. The Spirit of the Sea is … an unfortunate complication; I shall deal with it as best I can.' He could only hope the unfortunate complication wouldn't be too much for him to cope with.

'I see,' said Father Ormerod. Pontius entertained the suspicion, if only briefly, that the Spirit of the Sea might be entirely real, and a genuine rival to the Spirit of the Sky, and Larus its stronghold. It would, at least, explain the isle being "unpermitted" as a subject for discussion.

Father Ormerod folded his hands and changed tack. 'And what of your young lady, Miss Cynthia? What have you said to her?'

Pontius felt his face burn at the recollection of *that* uncomfortable interview. 'I cannot ask her to share such an … uncertain quest. I have no idea what hardships, what hazards might await me.' Or, indeed, if anything at all might await him, he privately thought. 'I have released her from our engagement.' A simple, polite phrase for a horrid, painful thing. Pontius wondered whether to add a lame comment along the lines that such an eligible young woman would find a more suitable marriage partner in due course but decided against it. What he had done was pretty much indefensible.

'I see,' said Father Ormerod again, and stared Pontius down until he could only avert his eyes. 'Then there is nothing more to be said.'

There wasn't, Pontius thought. But, oh, at this moment, how he wished for a sign, something to show him that he was doing the right thing. He had greatly disappointed Father Ormerod, let the theological college down, let the very Spirit of the Sky down. He was throwing away an admittedly dull but assured future. And he had hurt poor Cynthia, cut her to the quick, humiliated her in front of her family and friends. It would be very helpful indeed, he thought, to know that it had all been for a good reason and wasn't purely a hopeless wild goose chase, a bit of self-indulgent nonsense. He felt the leap of faith turning into a pointless jump off a cliff into he knew not what ghastly chasm.

Father Ormerod was still waiting, still staring, still hoping his student might be diverted from this madness. Pontius knew it, and was on the very point of saying, 'Wait …' when his eye fell on a patch of dust on a pew. Shocking, he thought, automatically, I'll fetch a duster directly. But as he focused on it, he saw words clearly written in the dust. Should he draw Father Ormerod's attention to them? No. He'd simply be courting an angry accusation of putting them there himself to support his decision. He couldn't prove otherwise, and it would only make things worse.

Father Ormerod eventually turned away, letting his hands fall by his sides. It was a gesture of defeat. 'I wish you well, my son,' he said sadly, and walked away.

Pontius, equally sad, was left to contemplate the words in the dust. They read, "Larus waits".

The Talkative Mr Bliss

It was a very sad Reverend Pontius that packed his possessions. He had been happy in his time at the theological college; he had not been by any means a star student, but he had enjoyed its ordered world. He had enjoyed the company and confidence of Father Ormerod, too, and had looked forward to a modestly successful future. Instead, here he was setting out to goodness-knows-where in search of goodness-knows-what.

Most of his books he regretfully left behind; they were too heavy to carry. He had asked his landlady to store them for him, saying he would send for them at a future date. When she had asked where she should send them, he was unable to answer. The sense of sheer folly was unbearable.

He had sold his silver shoe buckles to finance the journey. They hadn't fetched as much as he had hoped and provided only a small purse-full of money. He suspected that even with careful budgeting it wouldn't go far. Or not as far as he needed it to go, anyway. It was just one more uncertainty, one more point of unpredictability to deal with.

So, at last he found himself standing outside the front door with a bag and a bundle at his feet, and no idea in his head of how to begin.

'Bliss, sir,' said a voice.

'Eh?' said Pontius.

'Bliss is me, sir. That's to say, I am Bliss.' The owner of the voice gave an extravagant bow, and then had to reorganise his shabby coat and even shabbier waistcoat.

The necessity for a polite reply made Pontius bow in return and murmur, 'I give you good day, Mr Bliss.' Whoever you are, he thought privately, I wish you'd go away. It was annoying to be interrupted at such an important moment, but Mr Bliss showed no sign of going away. Indeed, he was smiling and waiting expectantly, his head on one side.

Aware that half an introduction had been made, Pontius began, 'I am ...'

But Mr Bliss got there first. 'Oh, you is being the Reverend Mr Pontius. I know, I know. And you are leaving now, aren't you?'

'Do I owe somebody money?' asked Pontius, desperately thinking there must have been an oversight. The last thing he needed was someone pursuing him for debt.

'Oh dear,' said Mr Bliss, laughing, 'Oh dear. No, sir. I am not the bailiffs, but I have been sent for you, y' see, to accompany you.'

'Accompany me where?' asked Pontius, hardly knowing whether to be relieved or puzzled.

'On y' journey, o' course. Isle o' Larus, I think was mentioned. Am I right?'

'Oh,' said Pontius, 'Yes. But who sent you?'

'Oh, my goodness; no, I can't tell y' that sir,' said Mr Bliss. 'Can only say by someone who thinks you're not fit to be out on your own, not with the wide world being what it is.' He leaned in alarmingly close and added, 'I'm t' be your guide and your help, y' see.'

Pontius had no idea what to make of this. It wasn't that guidance and help wouldn't be welcome, but he had grave doubts as to whether this fellow would be capable of anything of the kind. Had Father Ormerod engaged the man to accompany him? It was possible but if that were true, was he a guide or was he a spy? Or a keeper?

'I can't pay you.' It was the best Pontius could think of in the hopes that it might get rid of him.

'Bless you, sir! Already paid, I am. At y' service for as long as y' need me.'

Pontius stood with his mouth open, unable to think of an answer.

Mr Bliss waited, smiling happily, and then ventured, 'May I ask which direction you were thinking o' taking, sir? Could I suggest to the westwards? That is y' very best bet in this instance, being the nearest way t' the sea.'

'I know!' said Pontius, testily. 'Larus. An island. It'll be in the sea.' If it's anywhere, he thought privately.

This demonstration of wise logic made no impression on Mr Bliss, who merely said, 'Well sir, then lead on, if you please.'

Pontius remained rooted to the spot for the simple reason that he had no idea which way was westwards, not really. It wasn't something he'd taken much notice of. He looked up at the dull sky, seeking a non-existent sun.

'This way, sir,' said Mr Bliss, and proceeded to take Pontius firmly by the elbow and point him in the right direction. 'Shall I take your bag, eh?'

Mr Bliss was full of 'Shall I's; 'shall I hire you a mule, sir?' 'Shall I call you a carriage, sir, and hang the expense?' 'Shall I cut you a stout walking stick?' 'Shall I fetch you a pasty to eat as you go, sir?' 'Shall I rescue the shoe what has just fallen out of your bundle, sir?' 'Shall I re-tie the bundle more secure?' The solicitous questioning, so kindly put, was driving Pontius mad before the first hour was out. He needed to think, to consider how he might get out of the clutches of this man, and the constant chatter was distracting.

'Mr Bliss,' he said. 'May I speak frankly?'

'Certainly, you may, sir; at y' service at all times, as I said.' Mr Bliss was hoisting up the bundle, now tied with a knot that wouldn't have disgraced a seagoing man. 'Speak as frank as y' like.'

'Thank you.' Pontius looked into the man's face and saw nothing but solicitude. Either he was a genuinely good person, or he was a very good actor; it was impossible to tell which. 'Mr Bliss, I did not ask for you, or anybody, to accompany me on my journey, and I would prefer to undertake it alone. You have been recompensed for your trouble, you say, so if it's all the same to you, I'd like to dismiss you from my service. I do hope you understand. Nothing personal. Now, give me my bundle and go back to town. I'll continue as I intended. My thanks for your help. Bless you, Mr Bliss, and farewell.'

Pontius had said this with as much authority as he could find. Would it be enough? Well, yes, indeed; Mr Bliss handed over the bundle, smiled, bowed, and began to walk back the way they had come. Pontius stood and watched him stroll down to the bend in the road, where he turned and waved cheerily before vanishing round the corner. The sudden quiet, Pontius thought, was, well, *blissful*. It had been a little too easy, though, and as Pontius walked on he peered over his shoulder frequently, half-expecting the ebullient Mr Bliss to reappear. But there was no sign of him. Perhaps he really had been sent along purely as an assistant, and not a spy after all. A spy would not have given up and gone home following a polite request, now, would he?

Left with his own thoughts, Pontius began to wonder just how far he might have to walk to reach the sea. He had only the haziest idea. Perhaps Mr Bliss had been right in suggesting the hire of a mule.

'I am like a runaway child,' he said aloud, 'leaving home after a spat with his mother, with nothing but his dinner wrapped in a red spotted handkerchief tied to a stick.' Except he lacked the stick. And the dinner. 'I have been a fool. I am all unprepared.' What was it Mr Bliss had said, about him not being fit to be out on his own? That was insulting and cheeky but just possibly true. Would he be begging his dinner and sleeping under a hedge tonight? Was that to be the pattern of his life, of his great adventure, his vocation? What could he do to keep himself? Could he offer to preach and hope grateful people would look after him? The sparse congregation at his chapel had mostly fallen asleep. And it wasn't *his* chapel anymore, was it? He had given it up; thrown it away, according to Father Ormerod.

It was all very well going to seek your fortune, or your *vocation* if you wanted to call it that, but you still had to eat. It was all very worrying.

The hours trudged on and so did the Reverend Pontius, beginning to regret the weight of his luggage. It had seemed so little when he packed it. Had he made the most frightful mistake? Was it too late now to follow Mr Bliss back to the town, to say it had all been a terrible error of judgment, or to prostrate himself before Father Ormerod and beg forgiveness for this youthful foolishness? Was it too late to get back the little church with the somnolent congregation? Had his landlady already found another tenant for the room with the slightly damp bed? Surely, if he turned back now, he could set everything straight, couldn't he? Forget all the Larus rubbish and start again. All he had to do was make the decision.

'I shall.' Pontius said aloud, 'I shall turn back.' Except that he couldn't. His feet wouldn't move. 'What the …?'

Well, the fact is, his feet were moving, but only downwards. He had been so absorbed in his thoughts he had not paid attention to where he was going and had walked into a quagmire. He was sinking fast. What to do? They say you shouldn't struggle. Pontius struggled. It only makes you sink faster. Pontius sank faster. Up to his knees. Up to his waist. They say you should spread your arms sideways. Pontius lifted his bag and bundle above his head to keep them clear of the stinking mud. He sank faster still. Was this how it all ended? Up to your neck in muck?

'Don't struggle, sir. You'll make it worse.'

Pontius swore horribly: words he had hardly been aware of knowing, bellowed at full volume. He simply couldn't help himself. Things really couldn't be much worse.

'I didn' hear that, sir. Not a word of it. Ears quite closed, sir, to the unfortunate remarks of a man o' the cloth in difficulty. Quite forgotten already. Now, if y' would be so good as to pull one of your arms free and catch this ...' Mr Bliss was unwinding a coil of stout rope and preparing to throw it. 'I said to myself, "Bliss," I said, "there's a quagmire up ahead, and that Mr Reverend, he'll be straight in that quagmire, plop; you see if he don't. Head in the clouds, he is. Not a practical sort o' gent at all," I said. Try to keep the mud out o' your ears, sir, 'tis tricky to extract. That's the way. Hold on to the line, if y' please, now.' Pontius took a lunge at the rope and missed. 'Nearly there,' said Mr Bliss encouragingly. 'One more try, if y' will. There, now hold on tight and I'll 'ave you out in a tick. "No," I said to myself, "Bliss," I said, "go back to town and fetch a length o'rope, come back speedy-like and follow 'im." Try not to eat the mud, sir, it'll spoil y' supper something terrible.'

Mr Bliss had the line round a tree now and was hauling happily. Pontius emerged slowly, gasping, and thinking that there was nothing like a brush with death to concentrate the mind on the things that really mattered. 'I'm damned if I'll give it up!' he spluttered.

'That's the spirit, sir,' said Mr Bliss, 'forgivin' you the language once again. Just call me cloth-ears. There we go. Now, give me y' hand and we'll have you out o' there.'

Moments later Pontius was beached on solid ground, covered from head to foot in thick, dark, evil-smelling mud.

'Not to worry, sir,' said Mr Bliss, thumping him on the back. 'There, there. Spit it out. Nothing that won't wash off. I'll just retrieve your luggage; it ain't quite sunk yet.' And he set to work with a long stick, fishing for the bag and bundle.

Merry Serpents

An hour later, Pontius was installed before the fire in a nearby farmhouse, wearing nothing but a blanket and being fed nourishing chicken broth by the farmer's wife. At least, she said it was nourishing. Pontius couldn't taste anything but the foul mud that had got into his stomach. Mr Bliss had confiscated every stitch of muddy clothing and had carried it off with assurances that it would "all come off, dear me yes, and be good as new. Just leave it to Mr Bliss." Pontius didn't think he had much choice. Besides, the fireside was soothing, and he was feeling quite drowsy.

Odd, isn't it? Pontius thought. Not twenty-four hours into his great quest and he had already been practically kidnapped by the talkative Mr Bliss, possibly on the orders of Father Ormerod, no way to be sure. He had decided to abandon the whole thing and go home but had fallen into a quagmire before he could put that decision into action and been forcibly fished out again. And now here I am, he thought, stark naked save for a blanket, being force-fed mud-flavoured soup. It wasn't the sort of outcome he had expected. Questions filled his mind: was every day going to be like this? Could he cope with it if it was? Did he really have to eat any more of this soup?

'Thank you, madam,' he said, 'Thank you kindly but I think I have had enough.'

The farmer's wife nodded and took the other chair at his side. To his horror, Pontius realised he was expected to make conversation. What was he to say?

'Tell me, do many people fall in the quagmire?' It was all he could think of.

'Well, to tell the truth, sir, no. Most of 'em walks round it, you see. It's mostly mules that falls in. Stupid animals. Not the sense of a grasshopper between a team of 'em. Oh, not that I'm comparing you to a mule, sir, and you a man of the clergy, too.'

That was the end of that conversation, then.

Pontius searched his brain for another topic. 'Have you lived here long?'

'Oh, yes, sir. A long time. And my mother before me, and her mother before her.'

'Indeed?' said Pontius, trying to sound far more interested than he felt. With any luck she would rattle off her entire family history and he could safely have a little sleep while she did so. His eyelids were so heavy, the fire so pleasantly warm that even the chicken soup was feeling like a blessing, as it dissolved the lumps of mud in his stomach.

So, he dozed, and she talked at length about her life and family, not seeming to mind greatly whether he listened or not. Her husband was away in the fields, she said, and she was glad of the company, not adding, 'even if it is a muddy clergyman asleep in a blanket.'

It was when she reached back to the fourth generation that Pontius woke up, when his ears and brain understood something. What was that she had said?

'I do apologise, madam,' he said, 'I missed that last thing. Would you be so kind as to repeat?'

'Oh, sir, I merely said that my fourth-back grandfather were a seagoing man. I hope it doesn't upset you?'

'No, no,' said Pontius hastily, sitting up a bit straighter, taking care not to drop the blanket, 'not in the least. Do tell me more.'

She happily launched into the sketchy details of the seagoing man's life, while Pontius' mind was whirring. A sailor? Might he have said anything about the Isle of Larus? It was worth an enquiry.

'Larus,' he said, getting straight to the point. 'Did your forebear ever visit it?' He was anxious to ask before Mr Bliss should return. It was Pontius' nature to trust people, but he was learning to be wary, and he wasn't at all sure about what motives Mr Bliss might have.

'You mean the Merry Isle, sir?' Well, that was one point confirmed. Larus and the Merry Isle were one and the same, then. 'Oh, there were tales in the family about that.'

'I should like to hear them, if you please,' said Pontius, trying not to look too eager.

The farmer's wife chuckled, 'They say it is a sea isle, sir, many miles to the west.'

That was promising. 'Yes?' said Pontius encouragingly.

'Oh sir, you don't want to be hearing foolish tales like that.'

'I do, I do!' said Pontius, nearly dropping his blanket.

'It's not a fit story for a man o' the cloth. Legends they are, and we're not supposed to spread 'em. My old father got in trouble with the minister, just for talking about that isle.' She gave him a look, filled with suspicion.

She imagines I've been sent to catch her out telling these tales, Pontius thought.

'Madam, I assure you I did not sink myself in a quagmire with the aim of making you speak out of turn. I have a, um, *scholarly* interest in the legend, and I have the full approval of my superiors to research it. I am not a tattle-tale.' Blatant lies.

'Well, sir,' she said doubtfully, 'if the interest is *scholarly*, then I suppose I may tell you a little.'

Tell me a lot, Pontius thought.

'As I said, sir, my father's grandpa were a seagoing man, and he loved to tell stories of his travels in his later years. Now what he said, an' I'm not saying it's true you understand, what *he* said was it is an isle inhabited by sea serpents.'

Oh. Pontius' heart sank. It really was a legend, then.

'Great, huge sea serpents, sir,' she went on, 'and they're very partial to a sailor or two for their dinner. Very ferocious, sir. They leap into the sea, grab a sailor from a passing ship, gobble him up, and sit on the bare rocks of the isle to digest him. The belching is prodigious, they say. That's why ships won't go there. Can't blame them, can you, sir?'

'No, indeed,' said Pontius, losing interest. He had begun to learn that there were more things in heaven and earth than he had ever expected, but he drew the line at belching sea serpents. He settled back and closed his eyes.

'Still,' said the farmer's wife, ruminatively, 'they did say it was a pity that such an isle couldn't be approached. Has a wonderful harbour, all natural; that's what they said.'

She meandered on into the deeper reaches of her family history, leaving Pontius to wonder why that particular detail should be noted. Was it that the sea serpents used the good harbour to lure shipping in? Was that the point? It seemed an odd thing to pass down the generations, an odd thing in a legendary story.

When Pontius woke again he found his own clothes hung up and steaming before the fire. His shoes were propped up against the fire dogs. He was aware of someone moving about the room.

'Is that you, madam? How did ...?'

'No, sir, 'tis me,' said Mr Bliss. 'And if you're wonderin' 'bout the shoes, well, that mire do spit things back out that are lost in it, if y' have the patience to wait, which I do, so I have got 'em back for ye. Drying off nicely. I should look to y' blanket, young sir; you're displaying more than is seemly for a man o' the cloth.'

Pontius hastily covered himself. There was no sign of the farmer's wife. Had there been an opportunity for her to tell Mr Bliss about their Larus-related conversation? He hoped not. Truly, it was unlikely that she would be able to get a word in even if she wanted to. Not unless Mr Bliss had really been sent as a spy, and had asked specially, and given her the space to answer. The idea made Pontius very uneasy. I must watch every word, he thought. Secretly, he wondered about the Isle of Larus and its sea serpents and good harbour. If he discounted the serpents as nonsense, he was left with an isle far out in the western sea in possession of a useful harbour. But that would be well-known and well-used, wouldn't it? And not just a legend? Perhaps it just depends how far out in the ocean the island is, and whether it's on the way to anywhere else, Pontius thought. Or perhaps the people are especially unfriendly towards visitors but that didn't bode well for himself, did it? Pontius thrust the thought aside.

As they resumed their journey later, Pontius finding his left shoe wasn't quite dry, and Mr Bliss prattling away, it was difficult to think clearly.

'There is a trick, sir, to getting mud out of a clergyman's dark coat, oh, yes indeed ...'

Squelch, squelch, squelch, squelch, went Pontius' left foot as he walked. If Larus and the Merry Isle were one and the same, what was so merry about being eaten by a voracious sea serpent?

'Dabbing it with cow's milk is the usual practice, sir, but I don't agree with it, given the smell at a later date ...'

Squelch, squelch, cow's milk, squelch. Pontius' mind fell into step. Perhaps it's the serpents that are merry, rather than the sailors.

'Clay is better if you can get it, sir, draws out the dirt nicely. But not to be had round here ...'

Squelch, squelch, merry serpents, squelch. Perhaps, thought Pontius, the closer we get to the sea, the more logical the stories will become. At least he hoped so. Or perhaps it's that prankster the Spirit of the Sea that's merry. Except that it doesn't exist.

'So, I 'ad to extemporise, so to speak, sir, and use what *was* to be 'ad round here. A precious mix of dandelion extract and cats' urine. The cat was none too 'appy, I can tell you …'

'Mr Bliss, how long will it take us to reach the sea, do you think? A rough approximation will do.'

'Do depend how fast y' can walk, sir,' said Bliss, with admirable logic. 'But it is a fair way. Two weeks? Three? I 'esitate t' guess, sir.'

Three weeks of interminable prattle! It was a terrible prospect. Pontius stopped dead with a final squelch. '*What* did you say you'd put on my coat?'

The Other World

In the days that followed, the young Reverend Pontius was obliged to admit that Mr Bliss was a useful travelling companion. He found somewhere reasonable, both in price and in condition, for them to sleep at night. He seemed to know the way without being asked, and anticipated hazards, so there was no more falling into quagmires. Eventually, he insisted on hiring a couple of mules to carry their baggage and themselves.

Pontius was not a practised rider, and after the first day he announced that he preferred to walk at least some of the time. It was a choice between saddle-sores and foot-blisters. In the evenings Mr Bliss treated both afflictions with arnica and cheerful briskness. Pontius knew that, left to his own devices, he'd have drowned in the mire on the first day and never been heard of again, so he tried not to complain. He did have the occasional secret conversation with the mule, though, in which he let fly his frustrations at the bossiness of Mr Bliss. The mule would prick its long ears and attend with a wise expression, looking as if it were about to make a sympathetic comment. Anyway, it seemed to understand, and Pontius felt he had some sort of an ally.

But for all his chatter, Mr Bliss never said another word about the Isle of Larus, their nominal destination. Even when challenged directly on the subject, he was charmingly evasive and could happily speak for ten minutes on this tricky topic without actually saying anything at all. Pontius occasionally thought the fellow was wasted as a guide when he could have had an excellent career as a preacher.

It was true, too, that wherever they stayed, nobody else said anything about the legendary isle, either. Moving steadily closer to the Great Sea, Pontius had learned *that* much, its proper name, didn't incline people to know anything more about it, as he had hoped they might. So, to his disappointment, he learned nothing much as they went along.

He began to wonder, not for the first time, whether he had imagined everything; even the bits of writing. Most of the clues had indeed been written, and he wondered if he had unconsciously written them himself. That depressing thought was possible. Had he built up this whole thing as an excuse, seized on the Larus legend, as a reason to wander about the land? It was an uncomfortable thought and it depressed him through his barren journey. Right up until the moment he heard tell of the Other World.

'You are the Reverend Patience Pontius.'

How on earth did she know that? Pontius was already squirming with discomfort and ready to run for it. How had he let himself be talked into this? Consulting with a local wise woman. It was madness. The innkeeper's wife had made it sound so plausible, when he had enquired, without much hope of a helpful reply, about the Isle of Larus. She didn't know, she said, but why not ask Mistress M, as if everyone knew who this was and what she did. Pontius had said he had no idea who this lady might be and caused a chuckle or two in the bar. Well, people said, she might think she's a lady, but most of us wouldn't agree. The innkeeper's wife had shushed them and said that Mistress M had a very good eye for the future. Pontius had taken this to mean she was a fortune-teller, and said, 'no, thank you, if it's all the same to you.' Clergymen and fortune-tellers didn't tend to see eye-to-eye. Father Ormerod would have had an apoplexy at the idea of consulting such a person. 'No, no,' said the innkeeper's wife, 'Mistress M is very wise, has knowledge of all things, heaven-and-earth, things that most people don't know about. And besides, she won't charge you much.' If Pontius were to be entirely honest, it was the possibility of knowledge on the cheap that had changed his mind since money was running a bit tight.

'Why is she called Mistress M?' Pontius had asked, 'Doesn't she have a proper name?'

''Tis all the name she needs, sir,' said the innkeeper's wife.

So here was Pontius, having been conducted to Mistress M's small cottage by Mr Bliss, and forcibly plonked into a chair and then left to get on with it. She sat at her kitchen table, a woman so small and narrow, she looked as if a puff of breeze might blow her away.

He asked the obvious question, 'How do you know who I am?' It sounded foolish.

She stared at the tabletop as if it were the font of all knowledge. 'Your Mr Bliss told me so, sir.'

The obvious answer. How much more had Mr Bliss told her? 'Then you also know why I'm here.'

She ran her bony fingers over the tabletop, 'I know you are journeying to the sea, but no more.'

Was that to be believed? Pontius decided to cut through this to-ing and fro-ing nonsense. 'I want to know about the Isle of Larus.' There. It was out. She could answer if she wished, or he would bid her good day and leave.

She stared up at the cobwebby beams overhead for a moment, and then said. 'So, you do, so you do. But that isn't what I have to tell you, you see.'

'Eh?' said Pontius. Did she mean she wouldn't say anything until money had changed hands? He felt for his nearly empty purse. He hoped a very small coin would be enough.

'Never mind that,' said Mistress M, waving away the proffered coin. 'What I have to tell you is about the Other World. It's useful information, you know. It might scare you a little, but you'd do well to invest a half-hour in hearing it.'

Well, thought Pontius, if it's free, I might as well hear it anyway, even if it isn't about Larus. If it turned out to be gibberish, it had cost him nothing but a little time. He nodded to her to go ahead.

Mistress M placed her hands carefully on the table. She closed her eyes and Pontius closed his mind. Oh, he thought, in disappointment, one of those: a pretended trance. She is, after all merely a fortune-teller. A charlatan.

However, she got to the point remarkably promptly for someone in a trance.

'There is another world,' she said, all matter of fact. 'You can't see it or prove its existence, but it is there, nonetheless. And the things that happen there have an effect on our own world.'

'I refuse to believe in things I can't see or prove,' said Pontius, without thinking.

'Ah!' said Mistress M, opening one eye and laughing, trance or no trance, 'And you a man of the cloth, too. I thought that was just exactly what you did believe in.'

'That's entirely different,' said Pontius huffily.

'As I was saying, the Other World lives alongside this one, and has much in common with it, too. They mostly live in harmony, just now and then they intermix.'

'Intermix?' asked Pontius. 'What does that mean?'

'It means things can be seen, sometimes, by us of them, or by them of us. I believe the spirits make it happen for our own good.'

There it was again, multiple spirits. 'Do you mean the Spirit of the Sea?'

'Heard of that one, have you?' said Mistress M, 'Well, I understand any of the spirits can do it if they have a mind to.'

How many spirits was he being asked to believe in, Pontius wondered? 'I am in the service of the Spirit of the Sky. You can't expect me to accept these folktales as the truth.'

'You are very young, sir,' said Mistress M. It was a red rag to a bull for Pontius. No-one likes having their youth pointed out to them and used to undermine their conviction that they know pretty much everything already. He fumed in silence, trying to think of a suitably cutting response.

'Everyone is entitled to have their doubts, including you, sir,' she went on, 'but the Other World does exist, and it can have an effect on you. On all of us. I have seen it for myself from time to time. It is a very strange place, full of wonders.'

'I believe you are a charlatan, madam, making up stories to confuse the gullible,' said Pontius.

'Believe what you will,' said Mistress M, smiling, 'but truth is truth, like it or not.'

It was too much. Pontius jumped to his feet, flung the coin onto the table, bowed stiffly, and stormed out of the cottage, leaving Mistress M shaking her head behind him in that indulgent way older people always did.

He stomped off back towards the inn, preparing an un-clergyman-like earful for Mr Bliss. It had cost him a coin he could ill-afford to be told nonsensical rubbish about other worlds and ridiculous numbers of spirits. If word got round, every quack and charlatan between here and the sea would be queuing up with any story they could invent to sell to the gullible Reverend Pontius. It was insufferable.

He hadn't gone far when Mr Bliss appeared, as of magic, and fell in step beside him.

'How dare you leave me with that ... that *person*!' said Pontius. 'She is a mountebank ... a chiseller ... a ... a ...' words failed him.

'Unsatisfactory meeting, I gather,' said Mr Bliss. 'This way, sir, you are taking the wrong path ...'

'Unsatisfactory! She tried to spin me a yarn ... tell me a tale ... lead me up the garden path ...' words failed Pontius again.

'Garden path, sir, indeed. We need to retrace our steps, y' know, and you're 'eading for the river instead. Won't do, sir. Y' remember the bother we 'ad in the quagmire, I'm sure ...' Mr Bliss took Pontius firmly by the elbow and began steering him away from the water.

'You'd scarcely credit the things she expected me to believe,' said Pontius getting his preacher's hat on for a full-blown rant, 'other worlds, if you please. Other worlds and spirits that cannot be seen or proved!'

'Sounds right up your street, sir, beggin' your pardon, for a man of the cloth. Pray watch out for the cowpats ...'

'Don't *you* start, Mr Bliss,' said Pontius, treading squarely in a cowpat. 'The Spirit of the Sky is real and doesn't require proving. All these other things are quite different.'

'Different, sir, yes. Not to worry, I'll have your shoe smelling sweet as roses in a trice, sir. The splashes 'll come off your stockings, too ...'

Pontius had stamped in two more cowpats before he regained his presence of mind. 'I paid the old baggage, too, paid her good money for her nonsense.' It wasn't quite a lie, he told himself. More of an exaggeration. He had given her the smallest coin in his purse, and she hadn't even asked for that, to be fair. He felt himself calming down and his shoulders slumping. It was the sheer disappointment that had upset him. He so dearly wanted to know about the Isle of Larus, to prove to himself that he wasn't wasting his time, ruining his future career for nothing at all. It was becoming increasingly difficult to tell what was fact, and what was fiction and the contradiction was making his head ache.

'I apologise, Mr Bliss, for my ill temper,' he said quietly. 'It is not your fault I have suffered another disappointment. The truth is, money is running perilously low, and I fear I can't extend this journey, this quest, much further. Neither of us can live on air, can we?'

'Oh, sir,' said Mr Bliss, 'I told you right at the outset, at our very settin' out, that I've already been paid to accompany you. There's no need to be worryin' on my account, not at all.'

'Yes,' said Pontius, 'and I am grateful for it.' He truly was, at that moment. 'But I am speaking for myself. I cannot ask you to support me out of your wages.'

Mr Bliss stood with his head on one side, regarding Pontius keenly. 'It just so 'appens I have heard o' some work available, and not so far away from here, neither. Would y' consider takin' it on, sir, just to see y' through, money-wise?'

Pontius had an alarming vision of himself digging ditches.

'Oh, no, sir.' Mr Bliss seemed to share the inner vision. 'Nothing of the manual work.'

Pontius looked relieved but blank. 'Then what?'

'You is forgettin' sir, that you is an educated man. A man o' the cloth. Y' have skills, sir, in readin' and writin' and book-learning of diverse kinds. Those skills has values, don't y' know, sir?'

'What values? What do you mean?'

'I mean, sir, that there is a little chapel, just down-along in the village of Parchwell, that is lacking a minister. They have been without such a gentleman for a long while.'

'Have they not been sent another minister, then?'

'They have, sir, but he's a precious long time a-getting here. And they has had no proper weddings, or funerals, in the meantime. They would be mighty glad to 'ave a minister of the Spirit of the Sky, temporary-like, to do the necessary, preach a sermon or two and keep the records in good order.'

'How do you know this, Mr Bliss?'

'Oh, I were listenin' in to a conversation at the inn. So, I thought o' you, sir, straight away, and made enquiries. Discreet, you understand.'

'And they would ...'

'Pay you? Yes, sir. Not a lot, but it'd refill your purse a little, sir. What d' ye think?'

Pontius brightened up considerably. 'Well, I suppose it's in order to, er, help out for a small consideration.' He wasn't sure what Father Ormerod would say, but here was a congregation in need of a minister, temporary-like, and here he was, a minister in need of a congregation, temporary-like. It seemed like a happy solution for all concerned, but he wasn't about to do anything rash.

'Perhaps we could go and see this chapel, Mr Bliss, and perhaps talk to some of the people.'

'Straight away, sir, if y' wish. A most excellent plan!' said Mr Bliss, leaving Pontius wondering whether all these things were as random as they seemed, or whether he was being led along a pre-determined path.

Parchwell

Pontius had to admit it, he was happy. He hadn't expected much of the neglected congregation of Parchwell (despite the place sounding like a contradiction in terms, as he crossly pointed out), but he had fallen into place there quite naturally. Mr Bliss had run around being encouraging to begin with, but soon saw there was no need. The young reverend had jumped straight into the routine of regular services, sorting out the backlog of weddings, holding belated remembrance events and, most of all, tackling the jumble of paperwork. He had set himself to tracking down the details of births and deaths that had gone unrecorded, getting to know most of the parishioners in the process. It was a task he enjoyed tremendously.

'You have a real skill for detecting down the missin' bits, sir, if I may be so bold,' said Mr Bliss one morning. 'Oh, such a tangle it was, and you brought order to the chaos, sir. 'Tis a wonder to see the tidiness.'

'Why, thank you, Mr Bliss,' said Pontius. 'I enjoy it, that bringing order to things. By the way, I found another box in the crypt, behind the stone coffin. People are so ingenious at hiding things they don't want to deal with, aren't they? I'd be obliged if you'd give me a hand up with it. Still, I think it's the last one.'

'I will, sir. Just that one, then, and y' can leave everything in good order when y' go.'

'Go?' said Pontius. In all honesty, he had been so very busy and so happy in his work these last few months, he had not had time to think about leaving. Neither had he thought much about the Isle of Larus or the Spirit of the Sea, or any of those mysteries that had so intrigued him. The people of Parchwell had been so grateful, so welcoming, so helpful, and so downright glad to have him with them, that all those Larus-related things had been barged out of his mind by the onrush of practical matters to be attended to.

Parchwell was not a rich parish, but it had gladly provided him with a small cottage to live in and a small, regular stipend. Pontius had found he scarcely needed to spend the money, gifts of food were frequently left on his doorstep, so he kept a little of it and gave the rest to the parish's poor. He had endeared himself to them all, and for the first time in his life he felt like an accepted and cherished member of the community. With Mr Bliss to help, he had done wonders.

As the weeks had drifted into months, Pontius had become more and more settled. So, it came as a jolt to hear Mr Bliss mention leaving, as if it would definitely be happening, and to judge by the tone in which it was said, quite soon.

'There is still no sign of the replacement minister they promised, Mr Bliss. I had thought to stay until he turns up.' Pontius realised, that on some deep level, he rather hoped the replacement minister might *never* materialise. He couldn't desert the good people of Parchwell, could he? Even in his unofficial capacity he was doing some good, wasn't he? And that was why he joined the ministry in the first place. He was settled and happy, wasn't he? So why dig out all that Larus nonsense again? It made him uneasy and jittery to think about it, so why not stay, at least as long as officialdom permitted?

'I thought I'd stay,' he said, again, looking questioningly at Mr Bliss.

'Oh, 'tis for you t' decide, sir,' said Mr Bliss, with an uncharacteristic frown, 'but the winter will be comin' on soon enough, and you'll not be wantin' t' take any sea voyages then, for sure, sir.'

'Sea voyages?'

'Very bumpy and perilous in the wintertime, sir ...'

'What sea voyages?'

'Very bad for y' gizzards, sir ...'

'But ...'

'Terrible upsetting for the internals, it is ...'

'But I will stay here; won't I?'

'Even the most seasoned of sailor men fears a winter voyage in a rickety boat ...'

'What rickety boat? I'm staying here.'

'Otherwise ye'll have to wait right through to the spring, sir. And your isle is waiting.'

'I ...' Pontius stopped and stared at Mr Bliss. He remembered the message written in the dust, *Larus is waiting.* 'How do you know that?'

'Oh, everyone knows that your reverendness. See, y' have filled your purse here, and done much good while ye've been about it. But now, well, it's time to go.'

'Go where, Mr Bliss?'

'Why, to Little New Harbour, of course, sir,' said Mr Bliss, speaking as to an idiot. 'Where else? 'Tis the recommended place for sea voyages, as y' know, sir.'

Pontius didn't know any such thing, and didn't care for this sort of bullying, however gently done.

'Mr Bliss,' he said, as calmly as he could manage, 'I don't even know if the Isle of Larus is anything more than a legend, not really.'

'Well, then, sir,' said Mr Bliss, clearly stating the obvious, 'a seaport would be the very best place to find out, don't y' think? Now sir, if ye'll come down to the crypt, we'll rouse out that last box so y' can leave everything neat and tidy, eh?'

In the event, there was no further need to argue. Pontius had no sooner finished with the final box of papers than a message came to say the new incumbent of the parish was on his way and expected to arrive shortly. 'There, now,' said Mr Bliss, observing the stricken look on the reverend's face. 'Duty done, and all ready to hand over. I 'spect they'll be surprised to find it all in such good order, sir, don't you?'

Pontius imagined they would, given that the place had been left to go to wrack and ruin for so long. It was going to be a wrench to leave Parchwell and go back to that other life of wandering and searching. He had become fond of the parishioners, and the wandering suited him so ill.

'Very well, Mr Bliss,' he said, giving in to the inevitable, 'we will move on. But no more pointless stopping and starting if you please. We will go direct to … what do you call the place ... New Little ... no ... Little New Port ...'

'Little New Harbour, sir.'

'Yes, yes. Little New Harbour, and I'll enquire about the Isle of Larus and try to settle this once and for all. If there is no such place, we'll go back, and I'll ask Father Ormerod if he will forgive my errant ways and find me another little parish like Parchwell that needs a bit of sorting out.'

'And if Larus *do* turn out t' be a real place, sir?'

Pontius hadn't quite thought that far into the plan. 'If it is ... if it is, and I can get there, I'll see what they have to say about it and decide what to do with all proper information at my fingertips, Mr Bliss.'

'Will you go there, then, sir?'

'I may do.' Pontius was being careful not to reveal to Mr Bliss just how strong the call of the island was becoming to him again.

Not quite careful enough, for Bliss gave him a twinkly look, very reminiscent of Father Ormerod in the old days. The sort of look that said *you can't fool me, you know.* 'And what will you do there, sir, if y' should find y'self setting foot on its shores?'

'I will take the Spirit of the Sky to the people.' It was the best answer Pontius could give, just then. 'I can't imagine I'd be much use in any other capacity.' It was an unguarded comment, and he regretted it immediately. It was necessary to keep at least a veneer of confidence in place.

'And will the people be wanting that ministry, do y' think, sir?'

'To tell the truth, Mr Bliss, I don't know.' There were an awful lot of questions he could ask himself that would have the same answer.

Cast Adrift

The journey to Little New Harbour had been long and sad, at least for Pontius. His heart clenched each time he remembered his farewells at Parchwell, and each time he found himself thinking, from sheer force of habit, that it was time he visited the poor, or settled on a subject for this week's sermon. Sometimes he considered writing the dullest sermon he could think of and insisting Mr Bliss listened to it. This would be in revenge for Mr Bliss being so relentlessly cheerful while they travelled. But he never did it, of course. It wasn't really in Pontius' nature to be vengeful, but it did give him a degree of comfort to think about it. He wondered if the Spirit of the Sky would disapprove of this. The deity, as always, had nothing helpful to say on the matter. Or on any other matter. Pontius had felt useful, if nothing more spiritual, at Parchwell. Now he felt cast adrift again in an empty sea. He had no idea, really, whether that sea might contain the Isle of Larus. Finding the isle, as his conversation with Mr Bliss had revealed, might raise many worse problems than not finding it.

The landscape between Parchwell and Little New Harbour was a deserty sort of place, with scattered farms and not much else. They saw few people, and Pontius never said a word to any of them about Larus. He would save his questions for the seaport, where at least, he hoped to get a definitive answer. Is it out there or isn't it? Yes or no. No more fairy tales or misleading nonsense. Just the truth.

Pontius simply longed to be settled, to get on with the business of doing good and being useful. That much at least was clear to him. At times, he had the distinct and uncomfortable feeling that he was being taught a lesson, that his sojourn at Parchwell had been a preparation, rather than an end in itself. At other times he ticked himself off for over-thinking things. These things were just chance, weren't they? He was a minister of the Spirit of the Sky, carrying his ministry to the Isle of Larus. And if that place didn't exist, well he would carry it somewhere else, that was that.

Sometimes, late at night, he thought long and hard about what he had set out to do. It was that *who am I?* question that had brought him this far, after all. He had learned a good deal about *what* he was, Parchwell had answered that beautifully, but he still didn't know *who* he was, did he? Perhaps, he thought, this is something you only learn over the course of time, and I am being too impatient for an answer. If that should be true, then surely his lengthy search for the Isle of Larus, and the uncomfortable side-issue of the Spirit of the Sea, were unlikely to help very much. And the whole thing was nothing but a hopeless wild goose chase. The thoughts chased themselves round and round his head and left him grumpy and ill-rested in the mornings.

It was the scent that reached him first. Pontius stopped in surprise, sniffing the air like a roebuck. It was such a sudden halt that the mule, idly ambling alongside, nearly trod on his foot.

'Something wrong, sir?' said Mr Bliss, still annoyingly cheerful.

'I … it's … I don't know.' Pontius sniffed again. What was that? So pervasive on the breeze, both familiar and yet wholly unfamiliar. 'What is *that*?'

'What is what, sir?' Mr Bliss was grinning, suggesting that he knew perfectly well what Pontius meant.

'Stop pulling faces Mr Bliss and tell me,' said Pontius testily, 'It's … savoury.' It was so savoury it made his stomach growl. What did it remind him of? 'Reminds me of potted meat.'

'Salty, would y' say, sir?' said Mr Bliss, still grinning.

'Ah, yes, *salty*. Oh.' Pontius felt a complete fool. He knew the sea was salty. Everyone knew that. 'I just didn't expect to be able to smell it, that's all. You might have told me, Mr Bliss.'

Mr Bliss gave an indulgent shrug. 'My 'pologies, Reverend. Should 'ave given you fair warning of a smell o' salt on the breeze, 'deed I should. Most neglectful.'

'Very well, Mr Bliss, there's no need to overdo it. It simply took me by surprise, that's all. We're close to Little New Harbour, I gather.'

'We'll be there just after dark, sir, if we crack on. Quite exciting, ain't it, the end of the journey?'

"Exciting" wasn't the word Pontius would have chosen, terrifying was closer to the mark. All questions would be answered, he hoped, one way or another, perhaps even within a matter of hours. Until the very last minute he wouldn't know if his quest to find the Isle of Larus would be the making of him, or a complete and ridiculous waste of time and energy. He really wished Mr Bliss would stop grinning in that knowing way; it was very disconcerting.

'Let's get on, then,' he said to the mule, which gave him a look of infinite indifference, and they set off at a brisk pace.

In the event, it was well after dark when they reached the seaport.

Mr Bliss, who always knew everything, promptly installed Pontius at an acceptably clean inn and disappeared to see to the stabling of the mules.

Pontius himself, dog-tired and footsore, had a bite to eat and retired to bed. All the questions could wait for the morning. Having arrived at Little New Harbour and found it a quite real and entirely non-mystical place, the streets smelling of horse-dung and offal like anywhere else, he was fully prepared to make a hasty about-turn tomorrow and head straight home.

15

Far Flung

The Reverend Pontius strode down to the quayside and had to stop and stare in amazement. 'Just look!' he murmured, so taken aback he hadn't even noticed he was standing in a pile of fish guts. 'Just look at all ... that!' He hardly had the words to describe it.

Through the harbour entrance he had his first sight of the sea, and my goodness, it was impressive. Bright shades of blue and green, so very beautiful, and sometimes capped with white. Pontius had never seen anything much larger than a ripple on a pond before, and the liquid motion of the sea, while it impressed him deeply, left him feeling distinctly queasy. Was he really going to go out there, on all that heaving water? It was so big; much bigger than he had imagined. All the way to the horizon. Nothing but water. All heaving about in a very unregulated way. He regretted all the bacon he'd eaten at breakfast. And the two eggs. And the toast with bramble preserve.

He had not been able to find Mr Bliss this morning. Where had the fellow got to? Well, never mind, he had thought, I shall go and enquire myself. He had not said anything about the Isle of Larus to anyone. Why not? Was he afraid of being laughed at? You surely don't believe in that there nonsense, do you sir? Figment of the imagination. The clues that had brought him to Little New Harbour were tenuous. Did people here believe in the Spirit of the Sea? Would they laugh if he mentioned that, too? Someone's been pulling your leg, Reverend. He looked at the sea and swayed with it, taking in its rhythms and sounds. A small boat appeared in the harbour entrance, and oh, how she was being thrown about on the waves. Pontius quailed at the thought of doing anything like *that*. Or not if he didn't absolutely have to, anyway.

Perhaps, he thought, perhaps it will be enough to have simply made the journey, though it had been anything but simple. I have learned a great deal, after all, about myself and about people, too, he thought. That's valuable, isn't it? I can take that with me, whether I stay here, or go anywhere else. I'm free, surely, to apply the useful things I have discovered. Won't they be equally useful anywhere? The more he thought about it, the more convinced he was that the whole Larus thing was nonsense. Perhaps it's just a bare rock in the sea; somewhere like that might gather legends in lieu of facts. People did dearly love a legend. Or a sea serpent. He just had to make sure, and the only way to do that would be to ask, here and now.

    Pontius looked around once more in case Mr Bliss might have helpfully materialised, but there was no sign of him. 'I'll just have to do it myself, then,' Pontius said, and headed for a shack with "Little New Harbour Shipping Company" scrawled over the door. Someone there could answer his question, or laugh him out of the door, as they might.

A person with more wrinkles than face was counting coins inside. Good grief, thought Pontius, if that's what the sea does to you, I'm better off avoiding it.

'Ah. Oh,' said the person, 'Oh, you've made me lose count. Never mind. How can I be of service, young sir?' He abandoned the coins, looked Pontius up and down, took in his clerical garb, and added, 'Reverend, is it?'

'Yes,' said Pontius, thinking, please just let's get this over with. 'I ... wanted to enquire about the Isle of Larus.'

He waited for laughter, or pity, but neither was forthcoming. The man turned, ran his fingers over a chart nailed to the wall, and said, 'Next boat leaves on Tuesday week. Want to book a passage, do you?'

You could have knocked young Pontius down with a feather.

Larus was a real place, then—a place you could *book a passage* to. All the mystical ideas he had entertained popped out like a string of shooting stars. He barely prevented himself from asking if he couldn't *book a place for an audience with the Spirit of the Sea* while he was about it.

'Can I?' he asked.

'Course you can, young sir. Reverend. Though quite what you might be wanting with it, I'm sure I couldn't say. Completing your travels, are you? Taking in the far-flung places? Well, you'll like it. Can't get much more far-flung than that Larus Isle. Would be better if they flung it a bit further if you ask me. Not that you did, sir, but I do like to have my four-penn'orth.'

'I am a minister of the Spirit of the Sky, taking my ministry to the Isle of Larus,' said Pontius, pulling himself as upright as he could in the face of these perplexing remarks.

'I wish you good luck with that, sir! Indeed, I do. Now, you can book your place on the boat this moment if you wish. It's never very busy, but you never know, do you? Maybe there's a whole flock of young ministers wanting to take the Spirit out to that lonely place.'

Pontius hoped not. He was pretty sure there would only be room for one. 'It has to be you,' said a voice in his ear, so he swung round. Nobody there unless the clerk could throw his voice. Pontius shrugged. He was becoming used to this sort of thing happening whenever he had doubts. He felt for his purse.

'Don't you worry, Reverend, young sir. Inexpensive passage since nobody much wants to go there.'

'Thank you,' said Pontius, and spread coins on the counter. Goodness, it really was inexpensive, he thought, when only a few were gathered up.

'There. 'Tis all done. Be here for the tide. Midday, Tuesday week. Passage for Isle of Larus aboard the *Piddock.*'

Pontius looked affronted. It sounded mildly rude. He wondered for a moment if the clerk had been making fun of him all along, and the thought showed on his face.

'Not to worry, sir. Named after a seashell, I assure you. What name shall I put on the manifest, sir?'

Pontius handed over his name feeling he had given a hostage to fortune. All he had to do now was prepare himself to go out on that roiling sea. In something called the *Piddock.* He hoped the boat might not be too small but hesitated to ask in case he didn't like the answer.

In the intervening days, Pontius took himself for many a long walk around Little New Harbour, often ending on one of the nearby headlands where he peered out to sea, taking in its sheer breadth. It looked endless. However hard he squinted he could see no trace of any island, even out to the horizon. How far was it to the horizon? Pontius didn't know, but however far it might be, Larus, he still hadn't *quite* convinced himself it was real, was out beyond it. He felt himself engulfed by fear of the unknown.

That aside, Pontius was quite enjoying his own company. With no Mr Bliss keeping up a constant chatter, it was pleasingly peaceful. Where was Mr Bliss, anyway? He hadn't returned, and Pontius hadn't sought him out. Perhaps they both needed time to themselves.

He could spend all day watching the sea while he waited for the appointed day of leaving: with boats coming and going, loading, and unloading, fisherfolk at work with nets and crab-pots, he found it refreshingly normal. He tried to take an interest in the rhythms of seagoing life. Anything he could glean on the subject would make him feel a little less ignorant, and he dutifully ate fish in the evenings, though he balked at the squid. I'll have to get used to it, he thought, if I'm to manage island life. But the squid—well, he just preferred it when his dinner didn't stare at him quite so balefully when he was eating it.

Apart from this, Pontius tried not to think too often of what the future might hold. It worried him too much. The sea, heaving even on calm days, worried him too much. And the thought of an island, an isolated place you couldn't simply walk away from, worried him even more. Pontius distracted himself. He thought of Father Ormerod, safe in his cosy study at the college, training another upcoming protégé, someone who wouldn't disappoint him. He thought of the college librarian, whose greatest worry in all the world was somebody with grubby fingers assaulting one of the precious books. He thought of Cynthia, of how he had left her crying in the blossom-strewn garden. Was she crying, still? Had she found someone else, someone sensible and responsible, who hadn't taken a madcap idea into his head to run away to find a non-existent place? Except that it wasn't non-existent, was it? Probably not, at least. He thought of the kind people of Parchwell, now settling down with their new minister. That was a fond remembrance, and he smiled when he thought of them all. And here he was, kicking his heels in Little New Harbour, waiting for a boat that would take him to a future in goodness knows where. His stomach lurched, day by day, as the time to leave came closer. Would he find Mr Bliss waiting cheerfully in Little New Harbour if Larus should prove a disappointment and he came straight back again when the boat returned? Or would he be left to wander his own way home? Pontius hated all this uncertainty. It upset his digestion and set his imagination racing off to all sorts of unpleasant places. And he didn't have much imagination. He longed for the whole wretched thing to be over.

Voyage of the Piddock

'Good morning to you, sir,' said the rough-looking man, bowing clumsily, when Pontius presented himself at the quayside on the appointed day. 'You would be ...' he consulted a scrappy bit of paper, squinting and running his finger over the list it held. 'Ah. The Reverend Pontius, yes?'

Pontius nodded but wasn't really paying attention. He was looking at the boat tied up at the quayside. That couldn't possibly be it, could it?

'I am Jonas, master of the *Piddock*,' said the man with evident pride. 'I'll get someone to take your luggage, sir, if you'd be so kind.'

A surly-looking sailor grabbed the bag and bundle, looked at them with mild disgust and flung them into the boat. Pontius' feeble call of 'fragile' went unheard. For a wild moment he wondered if this might not be ... what did they call it? A tender, a smaller boat to take you out to the much bigger ship, moored elsewhere. But a quick scan of the harbour revealed no likely candidates. Perhaps it was somewhere outside the harbour.

Jonas the boat master seemed to read his mind. 'Not to worry, sir. This here is the right *Piddock*. She is a very sound vessel, I assure you. You couldn't do no better, not to get to Larus. That's cause she's mostly the only one who goes there,' he added confidentially, and laughed. 'So, if you'd be so good as to step aboard, we'll be on our way. Tides wait for no man, y' know.'

Pontius closed his eyes in silent prayer to whatever deity might be listening, Spirit of the Sky, Spirit of the Sea; it no longer mattered. He needed all the help he could get. Before he could open them again, he had been firmly grasped and manhandled down onto the boat. 'Let me be a good seagoer,' he mouthed silently. 'Let me not be sick. Let me not be thrown down to the bottom of the Great Sea with this wholly inadequate boat. Let me get to Larus in one piece, and I will never ask for anything else ever again, I swear.'

He found himself parked in a corner out of the way, while two sailors tended the sails and ropes. As he waited, he prayed again that he might have the strength to endure this voyage into the unknown. That he might not regret it. That Larus might prove to be the mystical, magical place he had imagined. That this might not turn out to be a mistake on the grand scale. Soon enough, the boat was sailing out of the harbour, and beginning to ride substantial waves. Pontius didn't think much at all once that particular reality took hold.

It was odd, he thought later, the way Mr Bliss had simply vanished. Disappeared from the face of the earth. No one Pontius had spoken to at the inn, while he was waiting to begin his voyage, remembered seeing his travelling companion at all. He supposed that delivering him to the seaport had been the end of the job for Mr Bliss and that he had turned around and headed back home. Commission completed. It worried

Pontius, though, that Bliss had left him without so much as a word, and without knowing that he would be able to travel on to Larus. What would have happened if he'd found it was indeed merely a legend? He would have been left adrift in a strange town. It was a horrid thought.

'Never even came to bid me farewell,' Pontius mumbled grumpily. That was so strange for such a talkative person as Mr Bliss. He had disappeared. Pop! Very much like that fellow who had spoken to him in the chapel, all those months ago, and set him on his quest to find Larus. A very strange coincidence. But there were an awful lot of those about, these days.

Fortunately for Pontius, his stomach proved stronger than he had expected, and after a very wobbly first couple of hours, it had settled down remarkably well. The wind was coming from just the right direction, and they would make a reasonably swift passage, according to boat master Jonas. Just a few days, with any luck. The word "days" had thrown Pontius a little. He had not thought, or perhaps dared, to ask how long the voyage would be. The idea of being at sea in the dark had rattled him considerably. But in the event, he quite enjoyed it. A sea voyage, though it had its dangers, was a very mind-freeing thing to undertake, he found, even in such an inadequate vessel as the *Piddock,* and he spoke very freely with Jonas whenever he could.

'Well, young Reverend, sir, the thing about Larus is ye'll never be a local, like, not even if you stay there ever so long. Offcomers do visit, from time to time, like yourself. Sometimes they stay, but they'll always be *on* the Isle, not *of* it, if y'get my drift. Islands are like that, sir. They look in on themselves. Course they do. But they look out, too, to all the ocean and the four winds, and what they might bring. Can't be helped. And Larus more than most, as ye'll find. Tis a conundrum, sir, and no mistake. Could never fathom the place, m'self. Open and friendly, to all, the people are.'

'There are people, then,' Pontius murmured with relief. He had lain awake wondering if it might be nothing more than a barren rock, inhabited by nothing but sheep, and imagined himself abandoned on it alone. Punishment for the sin of pride, for defying Father Ormerod. A lonely rock, with none but sheep to preach at. Very fitting. But apparently not the case.

'Oh,' the boat master went on, 'kind of innocent, those Larus folks. Not much sense o' trade. Bare necessities. You'll see that for y' self shortly. Don't be expecting no luxuries, sir. But my goodness, they take care of their own.'

Having established to his satisfaction that there were people on Larus, Pontius wondered uneasily whether they could be expected to take him into their community without a fight. After all, he was attempting to bring a new deity to the place. That was scarcely going to be easy and might prove very difficult indeed. 'They won't ... throw me off a cliff, will they?' he wondered aloud.

'Bless you, no sir. The worst they could do would be t' ignore you.'

Pontus wondered if that might not be the worse outcome. To bring the ministry of the Spirit of the Sky to this place and end up preaching to himself. Not even a sheep to listen. A tolerated outsider, doing no good at all. The words 'I'll just have to make myself useful,' fell out of his mouth. Where had that come from?

'No doubt you will, sir,' said Jonas, chuckling. 'But see you make time for a few frolics, won't you?'

Pontius turned and looked at him sharply. There was that word again. *Frolics*. He wasn't here for frolics, he was here to work, to do some good in the world. He was here because the place had called him. He hadn't given up a steady future for a few frolics, he thought sternly. Or, at least, he hoped he hadn't.

As time went on, Pontius began to ask more practical questions. Where would he stay on Larus? Was there an inn?

'Bless you, no, sir,' said Jonas, chuckling. 'Nothing like that. 'Tis a very small place, y' know. Someone will take you in, though, I 'spect.'

'And I suppose there isn't a chapel?' And if there was, would he find someone else occupying it?

'Oh, no, sir. Spirit of the Sea don't need no chapels. People speaks direct when they needs to. No chapels out on the sea when ye're being blown about in a storm, is there?'

Pontius was aware that he hadn't properly considered the practical details of how he would set up his ministry—even if the people of Larus were prepared to let him. Would he have to build a chapel with his own hands? Could he? He had never dressed a stone nor sawn a plank of wood. Was he going to fail on these practicalities, and never mind the difficulty of getting people to accept a new deity? Was it all in vain?

To distract himself, he dredged up a question. What about the Other World Mistress M had spoken of? He had dismissed it out of hand. But since there was nothing much else to do on a sea voyage, he occupied his mind with it. Another world, one that could affect him. He'd never seen any evidence of such a thing, and never heard tell of it before, neither. But it was hardly the sort of thing Father Ormerod would have presented for general discussion. Was it something that merited investigation, or just a bit of old woman's nonsense? It was one more thing Pontius didn't know. He wasn't sure whether he was up to dealing with the metaphysical, so he decided to run it past the boat master and see where it led. There was nothing much to lose by it.

'Oh,' said Jonas, when Pontius recounted what Mistress M had said, 'you are all surprises, sir, and no mistake. You are too deep for me, I b'lieve.'

'You have not heard tell of this?' Pontius pressed. 'Do you think she made it all up?' He didn't know, as so often, whether to be disappointed or relieved.

'Well, sir,' said Jonas, 'a man in my position, I hears travellers' tales, o' course, as I goes from port to port in the dear ol' *Piddock*. But y' can't set too much store by 'em.'

'Such as?' Pontius wasn't about to let this go, not now.

'Well, I met a travellin' man once who told a tale of monstrous things appearing out o' the air, sir.'

'What sort of things?'

'Oh, things he couldn't put no name to, sir. Things not he nor no one had ever seen the like of. Hard to put a name to somethin' ye've never seen before, as y' can imagine. That traveller, he went white as a winding-sheet when he spoke of it, sir. But then, he were four big pots of ale down at the time. Whether what he saw was your wise-woman's Other World, I couldn't say. But y' did ask, sir.'

'I did. Thank you, Mr Jonas.' Pontius doubted if this tale were anything more than drunken bragging.

'Oh, and one more tale, Reverend. There was a story I 'eard once, of a sailor who disappeared, pop, right in front o' his shipmates. Into thin air, sir. Was gone a long while, they said, and then, pop, back he came. Eyes wide as soup-dishes, they said, and never spoke another word, long as 'e lived. Entertainin' story for a winter's night, but as I say, sir, I don't give no credence to that sort o' thing.'

Pontius was shocked. After all, he had for himself experienced somebody going pop and disappearing into thin air, in the aisle of his own chapel. *His* fellow had stayed disappeared, but all the same, it was a little too close for comfort, and he resolved not to say any more on the subject. In the end, he supposed, he just had to be ready for anything. Anything at all.

Larus Waits

On the third morning, Jonas called him over. 'There you are sir. Isle o' Larus.'

Pontius squinted. All he could see was sea. 'Where?'

'Far horizon, sir, you're lookin' the wrong way, now. Over here. See? That little grey smudge.'

It was, indeed, a very little grey smudge. 'Is that it?' said Pontius in disbelief. 'Just that little mark?'

'It'll look a bit bigger presently, sir,' said Jonas, chuckling again. 'What a landsman you are, Reverend, to be sure.'

Pontius looked at the grey mass on the horizon, such a small place in such a large sea, as it slowly advanced, became larger, more distinct, more real. Everything that had happened to him centred on this spot. Was it nothing but a rock, after all? Simply a different place to spend his time, however remote. In a week or a month, would there be anything left of the magical entity he had built up in his mind? Or was it all a delusion, as Father Ormerod had so plainly said? Pontius didn't know.

'Sea serpents,' he said, as much to himself as anyone else, 'I don't suppose …'

'Oh, don't you be worryin' y' self about them, sir. That was a tale the Larus folks spread about in the long-ago. Kept the curious at bay, y' see, kept the pirates out. They'll never admit it, mind. They'll tell you the serpents is extincted, that's what they'll say if you ask.'

'And who should I ask? Is there a person in charge?' Pontius realised he had no idea how the place was run, or if it was run at all.

'Why, sir,' said Jonas, addressing him as if he were an ignorant child, 'It's not a person.' Pontius wondered for a mad moment if it were indeed run by sheep.

'No, no, sir,' Jonas went on, chuckling. 'It's a they.'

That didn't seem to make any sense at all to Pontius. 'What's a "they"?'

'You misunderstand me, Reverend,' said Jonas. The two sailors were laughing now and shaking their heads at the perplexed look on Pontius' face. '*They* is the four guardians. One for each direction, sir, north, south, east, and west. They run the isle together. Proper spats they 'ave, too, sometimes. They say you can 'ear 'em shouting and quarrellin' from miles off.'

Four leaders to deal with, to endear himself to? Pontius hadn't bargained for that. And quarrelsome, too. How was he supposed to keep four equally important people happy, to persuade all four to let him set up his ministry on Larus? And them all at each other's throats. It couldn't be done, could it? 'Four,' he said aloud, his heart sinking to the soles of his shoes.

'Well, no sir, beggin' your pardon,' said Jonas. 'Not just at present. They are one short. Only three, y' see.'

Pontius thought that only a minor improvement. 'Can they not choose another person, then?'

'Oh, they can't, sir. The Spirit o' the Sea sends 'em a new guardian when they needs one. They 'as to wait,' said Jonas, adding confidentially, 'and that Spirit takes its own good time, sir. Might play them a prank or two first. Does 'em good. But they takes it in good part, sir, and they know the new guardian will turn up in the end.'

'You believe in the Spirit of the Sea, Mr Jonas?' Pontius just had to ask. It was a bit of a blunt question, but he needed to know.

'I'm a seagoing man, Reverend. O' course I believe. Seen its merry pranks for myself, I 'ave. Took the top 'alf o' my mast clean off in a squall! That Spirit do dearly love a squall. Y' can hear it laughin' in the wind, sir, should y' survive the experience.'

Pontius had the frightful thought that he himself might be one of the Spirit of the Sea's merry pranks. Was that why he was here, why he had heard the call so clearly from the Isle? A minister of another spirit, dumped on their island, and left there, to create confusion, to see what the comic possibilities were? His heart sank clean through the bottom of the boat this time. If that is true, he thought, I am nothing but a joke. And what will become of me when the humour wears thin?

As they approached the large natural harbour of Larus, Pontius prayed desperately to the Spirit of the Sky for guidance. He could, after all, easily raid his purse to pay for a return passage to Little New Harbour and sit among the casks of salt fish the crew had come to collect, deciding what to do next. Or he could brazen it out, refuse to be made a practical joke by the Spirit of the Sea, and bring his mission to the island as he had intended. Should he go ashore for a while, seek out one of the guardians and discuss it? There would be time for that. He wasn't entirely sure he yet believed in the Spirit of the Sea, but these people did, and that was what mattered. Could he handle the contradictions of two deities? Was that the test he was being set? Oh, he thought, a clear sign would be such a help.

'There you are, sir,' said Jonas, with a sweeping gesture and a smirk. 'Larus waits!'

Thank you, Pontius thought, that is as clear a sign as I could hope for. Larus waits, indeed. He settled himself out of the crew's way, his heart thumping painfully in anticipation of what might lie ahead. A happy outcome? A bad outcome and straight off a cliff into the sea? He prayed fervently that something good might come of it all.

As the boat drifted into the quayside, Pontius stood up and looked. He hadn't exactly been expecting a reception committee, but there was nothing. Nothing except a small girl, sucking her thumb and watching the boat come in. She stared at Pontius, and he tried a hopeful smile. After a few moments, her eyes widened, and she picked up her skirts and ran, shouting, 'Mama! It's the *Piddock*! He's here! He's here at last!' Pontius could hear her still bellowing as she disappeared through a cottage door. 'The new guardian, Mama, he's here.'

In that moment Pontius knew the answer to the question that had possibilities were? His heart sank clean through the bottom of the boat this time. If that is true, he thought, I am nothing but a joke. And what will become of me when the humour wears thin?

As they approached the large natural harbour of Larus, Pontius prayed desperately to the Spirit of the Sky for guidance. He could, after all, easily raid his purse to pay for a return passage to Little New Harbour and sit among the casks of salt fish the crew had come to collect, deciding what to do next. Or he could brazen it out, refuse to be made a practical joke by the Spirit of the Sea, and bring his mission to the island as he had intended. Should he go ashore for a while, seek out one of the guardians and discuss it? There would be time for that. He wasn't entirely sure he yet believed in the Spirit of the Sea, but these people did, and that was what mattered. Could he handle the contradictions of two deities? Was that the test he was being set? Oh, he thought, a clear sign would be such a help.

'There you are, sir,' said Jonas, with a sweeping gesture and a smirk. 'Larus waits!'

Thank you, Pontius thought, that is as clear a sign as I could hope for. Larus waits, indeed. He settled himself out of the crew's way, his heart thumping painfully in anticipation of what might lie ahead. A happy outcome? A bad outcome and straight off a cliff into the sea? He prayed fervently that something good might come of it all.

As the boat drifted into the quayside, Pontius stood up and looked. He hadn't exactly been expecting a reception committee, but there was nothing. Nothing except a small girl, sucking her thumb and watching the boat come in. She stared at Pontius, and he tried a hopeful smile. After a few moments, her eyes widened, and she picked up her skirts and ran, shouting, 'Mama! It's the *Piddock*! He's here! He's here at last!' Pontius could hear her still bellowing as she disappeared through a cottage door. 'The new guardian, Mama, he's here.'

In that moment Pontius knew the answer to the question that had perplexed him, *Who am I?* 'Why,' said a voice in his ear, 'you are a guardian of the Isle of Larus, of course, what else?' There was no-one there when he turned, needless to say.

The Reverend Pontius stepped ashore into he knew not what.

THE END

Printed in the UK
by
clocbookprint.co.uk